The Distance from Here

ALSO BY NEIL LABUTE

Bash: Three Plays

Neil LaBute

The Distance from Here

a play

THE OVERLOOK PRESS
WOODSTOCK & NEW YORK

First published in the United States in 2003 by
The Overlook Press, Peter Mayer Publishers, Inc.
Woodstock & New York

WOODSTOCK:
One Overlook Drive
Woodstock, NY 12498
www.overlookpress.com
[for individual orders, bulk and special sales, contact our Woodstock office]

NEW YORK:
141 Wooster Street
New York, NY 10012

Library of Congress Cataloging-in-Publication Data

LaBute, Neil.
The distance from here / Neil LaBute.
p. cm.

1. Teenage boys—Fiction. 2. Suburban life—Fiction. I. Title.
PS3612.A28 D57 2003   813'.54—dc21   2002030826

Book design and type formatting by Bernard Schleifer
Manufactured in the United States of America
FIRST EDITION
10 9 8 7 6 5 4 3 2 1
ISBN 1-58567-371-4 (PBK)
ISBN 0-7394-3265-6 (HC)

For John Lahr

"O plunge your hands in water,
Plunge them in up to the wrist;
Stare, stare in the basin
And wonder what you've missed."

—W.H. AUDEN

"Oh well, whatever, nevermind."

—KURT COBAIN

PREFACE

I KNOW THESE GUYS. Well, maybe not "know" know them, but I *know* them.

The people that populate the landscape of *The Distance from Here* are very familiar to me, much more like the kind of folks I grew up around than the fairly privileged, white collar, white bread men and women I've spent the last few years writing about. Don't get me wrong, I know those people too, but the Darrells, Tims, and Jenns of this world hold a special place in my mind. A unique, uncomfortable space that says, "Damn, that could've been me." Even growing up in America, I think most of us are only two detentions and one dead-end job away from ending up just another failed dreamer with a difficult childhood and lousy luck. You make another couple mistakes, have a baby or two, start pulling down minimum wage, and you might be staring real trouble in the face. A fellow like Darrell, however, doesn't even have that chance. In high school, I sat next to a bunch of boys like Darrell and Tim in woodshop and algebra and study hall and watched them simmer and burn and consistently pull down a solid D– in nearly every subject. They knew, even at sixteen, that they had absolutely no hope in this life and they were pretty pissed about it. Pretty damn pissed indeed.

The Distance from Here takes a whack at capturing some of that teenage rage in a story about families. Shattered families, to be sure, but families all the same. The absent fathers that haunt the pages of this play are not the only "missing persons" here; emotionally, Darrell and company went AWOL a long time ago. Darrell, his friends, and the other characters of this story are banging their collective heads against the bars of their cage, not exactly sure whether they're trying to get out or to get back in. As people, I'd probably give them wide berth if we ran into each other in McDonald's. As characters, they make me laugh, they make me frustrated, they make me sad. They also make me wish I were a better person, which I guess is saying something.

When I was in high school in Washington State, there was a myth that ran through our hallways; our own little urban myth, in fact, about a boy and girl who had dated since junior high. I still remember their faces. It was whispered that she had gotten pregnant on several occasions and, whenever it happened, the boy would pound the girl in the stomach until she miscarried. That story stayed with me for a long time, right up until I wove it into the dramatic fiber of this play. I hope it has finally left me now, a part of this world and no longer a frightening image from my teen years. I think that is often why writers write and painters paint and musicians play their instruments. It's not just because they have a gift, but also to create something even slightly more beautiful or coherent or illuminating than the frenzied, scrambled memories of their own pasts. *The Distance from Here* is some sort of effort on my part, then, to acknowledge a kind of person I've always known well but consciously and constantly marginalized. I never liked the way those kids dressed, or the music they listened to, or the way they talked, so from the beginning they were, in essence, dead to me. This is my attempt at a resurrection.

The Distance From Here was first performed by the Almeida Theatre Company on May 2, 2002. It was directed by David Leveaux; the set design was by Giles Cadle; the costume design was by Edward K. Gibbon; the lighting design was by Mark Henderson; the sound design was by Fergus O'Hare; US casting was by Daniel Swee; UK casting was by Fiona Weir; the fight director was Alison de Burgh; the production manager was Paul Skelton; the company manager was Rupert Carlile; the company stage manager was Maris Sharp; the deputy stage manager was Sophie Gabszewicz, the assistant stage managers were Helena Lane-Smith and Simon Wilcock; the costume supervisor was Edward K. Gibbon; wardrobe supervision was by Meg Lawrence; Almeida artistic directors: Jonathan Kent and Ian McDiarmid. The cast was as follows:

Darrell	Mark Webber
Tim	Jason Ritter
Cammie	Amy Ryan
Shari	Ana Reeder
Rich	Enrico Colantoni
Jenn	Liesel Matthews
Girl	Malaya Rivera Drew
Boy	Joshua Brody
Employee	Alan Sayce

SILENCE. DARKNESS.

THE MONKEY CAGE

Thick steel bars surround a dusty replica of an African landscape. A large
PLEASE DO NOT FEED THE ANIMALS! *on a metal sign.*

Two teens stand near the exhibit, peering through the bars. Both about
seventeen. Concert T-shirts, baggy jeans, Nikes. DARRELL *has long hair*
and cunning eyes. He'd have an angel's face if not for the downward twist
his mouth makes. TIM *is taller, with a softer look about him altogether. Not*
muscular yet, but carrying plenty of bulk.

TIM *scratches at his leg, lost in thought, while* DARRELL *tosses the last of*
a candy bar into the cage.

DARRELL

—fucking apes, huh?

TIM

Yeah.

DARRELL

They gotta be so *cheery* about?

TIM

Dunno—

DARRELL

Shitting up their cage, eating all sorts 'a *tropical* crap give you
the runs your whole life through—

TIM

Uh-huh—

DARRELL

And filthy little babies hanging from your backsides . . . 's a *bullshit* life! 12 x 12 pen's your kingdom and you don't know shit about <u>whatever</u>.

TIM *leans forward, scratching and studying the animals.*

TIM

—they got nothing on us.

DARRELL

Wipe that smile off your fucking faces! (BEAT) *Ecstasy* for no apparent reason—

TIM

Yep.

DARRELL

Hey, lookit that one . . . hanging there, picking at herself like she's got a *lifetime* ahead of 'er. (*loudly*) Shoot a documentary on your ass, squeeze a couple kids outta you and you'll be a fucking *ashtray* on somebody's coffee table time the new year rolls around! Stupid ass chimp . . .
> (TIM *suddenly jumps back and pulls hard at his leg. He shakes the denim with fury and stamps at the ground.* DARRELL *looks over casually at his friend but waits a bit before speaking.*)
. . . fuck you doing?

TIM

Ants! Ants or something!

DARRELL

Come on, man—

TIM

Ouch! Fucking oww!!

DARRELL

Can't take you anywhere, I'm serious.

TIM

Crawling up my leg, for chrissakes!

DARRELL

Fucking *production number*—

TIM

Red ants doing at the zoo in <u>October</u>?!

TIM *dances about while* DARRELL *watches.*

DARRELL

They on your thighs yet? That ain't good—

TIM

Scratching my ass off . . . sue these fuckers for this, talk to my dad or something!

DARRELL

Call <u>St. Louis</u> about bugs? Yeah, your old man'd really get into some 'a that shit.

TIM

Fuck!

DARRELL

—then maybe he can chase you around the neighborhood with a hammer, like he used to.

TIM

He said "gimme a jingle ya need anything" smart ass! (BEAT) They're, like, hiding in the fucking seams, gonna pinch me for six weeks from now!! Damnit!!!

DARRELL *looks back at the monkeys again while* TIM *goes down on the sidewalk, clawing at his inseam.*

DARRELL

Don't worry about your fucking stone wash, man, they can crawl up your dick, make their way to the *prostate*, article I read once—

TIM

Up yours!

DARRELL

No, up <u>yours</u>, that's what I'm telling you.

TIM

Fucking pinchers! Awwww!!

DARRELL

I fuck you not . . . <u>Geographic</u> magazine or something, study in *Indonesia*, some country you can't find on a map you look for twenty minutes—

TIM

Fuck!

DARRELL

Not out to frighten you, hell no, but they crawl right <u>in</u> the hole, hang out in the folds 'til you doze off, they got a dozen ways to go about it, but climb right in and pitch a fucking pup tent knee-deep in your *testes*, later tonight.

TIM

That's bullshit!!

DARRELL

Wish it was, man, but it drove some dude half insane in, like, Sri Lanka. Ran through the bazaar and killed, maybe, forty guys or something with a *machete* . . . and they let him go. Yeah! 'Cause ants up your dick are some kinda legal hitch, most countries that part 'a the world—

TIM *now looks petrified. He glances about, then begins tearing his jeans off and pawing at himself.*

TIM

Fuck that!

DARRELL

I'll keep watch, tell ya if any girls are coming, shit like that—

TIM (*checking himself*)

—don't see any.

DARRELL

Nah?

TIM

The hell I'm so itchy for?

DARRELL

Don't know, Tim . . . not your conscience, so I dunno.
(*After a bit more scratching,* TIM *stands and buttons his fly.* DARRELL *waits until he is nearly finished.*)
Yeah, as long as you checked your thing we've got no problem. I mean, you did *examine* it, right?

TIM

Huh?

DARRELL

'Cause those little fucks are nothing if not cagey. (BEAT) I just don't wanna see you driven nutty, that's all . . .
> (TIM *sizes this idea up, then looks about. He begins pulling down his pants again, hunching over protectively in his underwear while examining himself.* DARRELL *watches, amused.*)

Don't worry, Tim, looks like the most *natural* thing in the world, take your time—

TIM

Shut up! You see any on me?!

DARRELL

Uh-uh.

TIM

Fucking red marks all over—

DARRELL (*pointing*)

That one on your calf?

TIM

Where?!!

DARRELL

Back 'a the knee—

TIM

Ahh, no. Birthmark.

DARRELL

All pink like that?

TIM

Yeah, since I was a kid—

DARRELL

That's *pretty*—

TIM

You fucker . . . (BEAT) Come on, you see 'em or anything? Fucking Hanes *underwear* in a public place—

DARRELL

Don't be ashamed. You got a legit beef with these guys, wear whatever the fuck you want—

TIM

Come on, help me!

DARRELL *leans forward, examining* TIM *a bit more intently.*

DARRELL

Nope—

TIM

Fucking ants. (*looks again*) Don't see nothing . . .
          (DARRELL *laughs to himself.*)
Just knock it off!

DARRELL

—so pull on your pants, then, you got no troubles. Look like
a fucking *homo*—

TIM

'Kay. You dick.

TIM *works at pulling his jeans back on over his shoes.* DARRELL *fires up a smoke.*

DARRELL

Let's blow this—

TIM

Yeah. (BEAT) You wanna go back for gym, last couple periods?

DARRELL

Fuck you think?

TIM

Right.

DARRELL

Head on over to the mall, if ya wanna—

TIM

Sounds good. Time you gotta be home?

DARRELL

Whenever—

TIM

Time your mom get in from work?

DARRELL

Two-thirty, three, something around there—

TIM

Oh. (BEAT) What about her boyfriend? He works over at the, what, Ken-L-Ration plant or somewhere like that, right?

DARRELL

I guess.

TIM

Time he come over? I mean, usually?

DARRELL

Hey, you taking a fucking *census* or something?!

TIM

No—

DARRELL

Kinda fucking *game show* shit is this?! Huh? I don't <u>gotta</u> be home no time—

TIM

Sorry.

DARRELL

Worry about it. You hungry or not?

TIM

Yeah.

DARRELL

Me too. Get us some eats, "International Food Fair." 'Kay?

TIM

Sounds good.

DARRELL

—means we get some <u>hot sauce</u> on a fucking burger, some *mexi*-fries—

TIM

Food's not bad . . . lot 'a tables, anyway.

DARRELL

It's okay. At least better'n the fucking joint you work at—

TIM

—hey, 's money.

DARRELL

Whatever. Fucking *Chink* food, Tim, that's stooping pretty low.

TIM

Uh-huh.

DARRELL

<u>Way</u> the fuck down there—

TIM

I know. (BEAT) Need some bucks, though, 's why I took it.

DARRELL *looks over at* TIM, *poking him with a finger.*

DARRELL

Whatever . . . (BEAT) You did check on the <u>inside</u>, right? I mean, pull it open and all? 'Cause I don't want you showing up at our place all hours with a fucking *cleaver* or that kinda shit—my mom's boyfriend'd kick your ass.

In spite of himself, TIM *laughs at this.*

TIM

I looked. I fucking <u>did!</u>

DARRELL

Good for you. (BEAT) Me, I could never do that, mess around down there, don't got the stomach for it. Feel like a total fag—

TIM

Just shove it.

DARRELL

All right, we're outta here . . . fucking *primates*, had enough for one day. Like my step-nephew, plays all fucking day, still don't get enough. I hate that age—

TIM

Which?

DARRELL

Little. I hate 'em when they're little.

TIM

—yeah.

DARRELL

Let's go check out the new Nikes, something like that.

TIM

Sounds good.

DARRELL

Whatever. (*toward the apes*) You got anything we can heave at these fuckers before we take off?

TIM

Nah.

DARRELL

Couple quarters? Maybe a rock?

TIM

No . . . I don't got nothing.

DARRELL

Ahh, fuck it. Let's go . . .
   (TIM *makes a sudden move and noise that scatters the apes and causes a frightening chatter.* TIM *and* DARRELL *smile at this.*)
Fucking *simians* . . . they just don't get it, do they?

THE LIVING ROOM

Well worn and threadbare. Not messy but cheap. Really cheap. Matching chairs and couch. TV in the corner, on and loud.

CAMMIE *stands drinking a can of Coke and smoking. Thirty-eight, she chooses clothing that makes her look younger, if a little foolish. Wears her hair long. She yawns loudly.*

SHARI *is on the sofa, sorting a few bottles of formula and the like in a soiled diaper bag. She is twenty-one, very thin and sexy, although her face is plain and almost sad. A baby cries in one of the other rooms.*

CAMMIE

—fucking pooped, huh?

SHARI

Yeah.

CAMMIE

And it's only hump day. Believe that? Still got two more to go—

SHARI

Uh-huh.

CAMMIE

How's the baby?

SHARI

'S kinda colicky.

CAMMIE

Yeah, poor thing. Keeping any milk down 'em?

SHARI

Little bit.

CAMMIE

He's gonna be all right . . . Darrell went through the same
thing. Worse, probably.

SHARI

Yeah?

CAMMIE

Shit . . . like he was gonna bust apart, screaming and crying
just like that, day after day. Drove me crazy—

SHARI

I know.

CAMMIE

I mean, God . . . you don't know what the hell to do! New
mom, middle 'a the night. You just feel like knocking the shit
outta them—

SHARI

Yep.

CAMMIE

—anything, just to shut 'em up.

SHARI

I know what ya mean. Sometimes I just crank the stereo and
zone out, you know, kick back and say, "fuck it," cry if ya
wanna, I gotta take a break—

CAMMIE

Right.

SHARI

—and I don't think that's so wrong or whatever, I really don't.

CAMMIE

Me neither. He don't die from it, does he?

SHARI

Exactly. Little hungry or wet himself, hey, so hold on a second. You grow up, you wait for shit all the time—

CAMMIE

Every day.

SHARI

Every day 'a your life, true, so I don't think you oughta just jump up whenever they start wailing like that . . . just teaches 'em bad manners, really.

CAMMIE

That's what it is.

SHARI

Seriously . . . and *false* expectations 'a things. 'Cause life isn't like that, with people all down on one knee for ya when you need 'em, just gotta cry out or say, "hey, I want this or that." 'S totally not that way at all—

CAMMIE

I agree. (*pointing at a bottle*) You want me to throw one 'a them in the microwave for ya?

SHARI

Nah . . . he likes 'em cold, fine. I mean, room temp or whatnot.

CAMMIE

'Kay.
        (CAMMIE *looks up at the sound of a car door.*)
Oh. Here comes Rich—

RICH *enters the house, swinging a lunch pail. Thirty-three or so, plain-faced but muscular. He looks at* SHARI *sternly for a moment, then walks over and kisses* CAMMIE *on the cheek.*

SHARI

Hey, Rich—

RICH

'S up?

CAMMIE

I, ahh, called Shari to gimme a lift home from work, hope that was okay.

RICH

Uh-huh.

SHARI

We didn't mind . . . nice to get out.

RICH (*to* CAMMIE)

Could've taken the Impala today.

CAMMIE

No, see, that's why I called her. Got a bunch 'a oil and stuff, dripping down.

RICH

What?

CAMMIE

Well, looks like oil . . . kinda reddish, but thick. 'S all over the driveway.

RICH

Fuck.

CAMMIE

You didn't see it out there?

RICH

No . . . (BEAT) Shit, just got it back!

The baby cries out; RICH *makes a motion toward* SHARI.

SHARI

Sorry.

RICH

'S fine. I mean, if it doesn't bother you—

SHARI

Right, yeah, I was just gonna—

RICH

'S a *baby*, they do shit like that. Cry.

SHARI

—I know, but—

RICH

You do? Huh. Well, that's something, I guess . . . at least you
know it.

A moment of silence between them all; the child whimpers.

CAMMIE

Anyway, that was nice of Shari, did me a favor—

RICH

Right. Yeah—

SHARI

No problem . . . we were planning on coming over tonight,
anyway. Bought a new video for us, that one comedy one.

RICH

Oh.

CAMMIE (*to* RICH)

Just to watch the tape. Not dinner.

SHARI

No, I'm gonna grab something on the way, I mean, unless—

RICH

—great.

RICH *pulls off his sweatshirt and moves to the sofa. He kicks back as he
fires up a cig. Grabs up the remote. Phone rings and* CAMMIE *picks it up.*

CAMMIE

H'lo. Yep. Uh-huh. Right. Oh well. Yeah. Whatever. No. Fuck no.
Nevermind. Fine. 'Kay. Later. (*to the others*) 'S just Darrell—

RICH

Fuck's he want, calling?

CAMMIE

Ride over to the *mall*.

RICH

Shit.

CAMMIE

I told 'em "no."

RICH

Good. (*to the remote*) The hell is . . . ?

CAMMIE

Cable's out.

RICH (*tossing the remote*)

Jesus Christ! Nice place—

CAMMIE

Hey—

RICH

You mail the bill or not?

CAMMIE

Yes, I mailed the fuckin' bill.

RICH

Well, then what's up?

CAMMIE

I dunno. You flip 'em on, you get snow.

RICH

Really?

SHARI

Yeah, anything above seven is fuzzy.

RICH

And you did the little wire thing in the back?

CAMMIE

Shit, Rich, do I look retarded to you?

RICH

Kinda—

CAMMIE (*smiling*)

Fuck you—

RICH

Forget it, you're too old for me.

CAMMIE

Prick.

RICH *blows her a kiss. She pretends to eat it.*

SHARI

—mine went out last week, too.

RICH

Yeah, but you can't afford cable.

CAMMIE

Rich!

RICH

What, I'm just saying—

SHARI

It's okay—

RICH

I just mean you don't <u>pay</u> for it, you had that neighbor guy
'a yours do that thing with the back 'a the box, that's all I
mean. It goes out you can't really be *weeping* about it . . . this
is different.

CAMMIE

Still don't gotta say it like that.

RICH

What?!

SHARI

Not a big deal.

RICH

Exactly.

CAMMIE

Anyhow, we still got all the other channels—

RICH

What "others"?

CAMMIE

The regular ones.

RICH

"Regular?" Only "regular" thing on the whole fucking tube is
Sports Channel—

CAMMIE

Listen to 'em. You got the ABC, CBS and NBC. Plus that PBS
thing—

CAMMIE *slides in next to him and takes a hit off his smoke.*

RICH

Oh, cool, that's fucking great . . . you think I'm gonna do, watch <u>Nova</u>? 'S not about *cars*—

CAMMIE

No. I'm just telling ya—

RICH

Whatever.

A moment of silence between them all. Only the baby crying.

SHARI

Ummm . . . could I get a drag, Rich?

RICH *nods and* SHARI *slips down on the other side of him. He puts his hand up and she reaches her mouth forward, sucking deeply off his cigarette.*

RICH

Well, ain't this just *cozy*?

CAMMIE

Ummm-hmmm—

They all giggle. CAMMIE *lays her head on* RICH*'s shoulder.* RICH *puts his free hand on her shoulder while keeping an eye on* SHARI.

SHARI

Hey. I got that tape in the car, should I go and . . .
        (*They both look over at* SHARI; *she stops cold.*)
. . . maybe I oughta take off.

RICH *gets back up, leaving his sweatshirt where it fell. He heads for the door.*

RICH

Worry about it . . . I'm gonna go pull the Chevy in the garage, take a look at it. You guys go back to your girlie shit or whatever—

CAMMIE

Oh yeah, that's us.

SHARI

Right.

RICH (*to* SHARI)

—or you might wanna go hold your kid a *second*, get him to fuckin' shut up. That might be something to do.

RICH *smiles and exits.* CAMMIE *looks over at* SHARI, *but neither one of them make a move for the baby.*

> CAMMIE

So—

> SHARI

Yeah.

> CAMMIE

—don't listen to that. He's tired.

> SHARI

Right.

> CAMMIE

No big thing.

> SHARI

'Kay.

> CAMMIE

—what tape'd you get, anyway?

> SHARI

You know. That one comedy one.

> CAMMIE

Oh, right. Good. That'll be good.

SHARI *slowly lays her head down in* CAMMIE's *lap.* CAMMIE *plays with her hair as* SHARI *closes her eyes. The baby continues to cry.*

THE MALL BUS STOP

Two wire benches near a great expanse of concrete retaining wall. Part of a logo sign overhead with a flickering bulb that reads INGTON GALLERIA.

TIM *and* DARRELL *lean up against the wall some distance off, smoking.* DARRELL *holds a drink.*

> DARRELL

—fucking "Arches," huh?

TIM

Yeah.

DARRELL

What's McDonald's doing, the middle of a *supposed* "celebration of international tastes," anyway, I ask you?

TIM

Dunno. (BEAT) Nothing happening out here . . . you wanna go back down the lower level, do something?

DARRELL

Sounds good.

TIM

Yep.

DARRELL

Grab us some more CDs maybe, I don't give a shit.

TIM

'Kay. (BEAT) I gotta be back some time, though, got an extra shift tonight.

DARRELL

Not asking for a weekend in fucking *Vegas*, am I?

TIM

No.

DARRELL

Jesus!

TIM

I'm just saying . . . just <u>saying</u> it, that's all.

DARRELL

I heard you. Fine. Hang out here, do some video, fine—

They pass the smoke a few times without speaking.

TIM

—so, we gonna go back in? I still got a little time—

DARRELL

"Time?" Oh yeah, I forgot, you gotta *work*—

TIM

Whatever.

DARRELL

—yeah. (BEAT) I told Jenn we might meet her out here, though.

TIM

Oh man.

DARRELL

What?

TIM

Nothing.

DARRELL

No, fuck that, alwaying *moaning* your ass off, she does anything with us. Fuckin' jealous or what?

TIM

—no.

DARRELL

'S my <u>girlfriend</u>, okay?

TIM

Uh-huh.

DARRELL

Jesus, Tim, you got a *woodie* for me or something, gay shit like that?

TIM (*smiling*)

Asshole.

DARRELL

Then what the fuck?

TIM

I just—

DARRELL

Didn't make no promise, anyway, okay . . . I said "maybe."

DARRELL *lights up another cigarette. Offers* TIM *a drag.*

TIM

—I don't like her so much.

DARRELL

Up yours!

TIM

I don't, though. Not anymore. (BEAT) She fucking called me "stupid" once.

DARRELL

Oh yeah, she was really outta <u>line</u> on that one—

TIM

That's not so funny, you know? Hurt my feelings, maybe, give a shit about me you might care.

DARRELL

Just shut up and finish the smoke. Mall's not open forever, ya know.

TIM

'Kay. (BEAT) She say she's coming for sure?

DARRELL

I dunno, just hurry up! (*sips his drink*) I'm outta Coke. Shit! Fucking thirsty—
> (TIM *takes another hit off the Camel Light as* DAR-RELL *sucks savagely on his straw, looking for moisture. He looks up suddenly, watching something.*)

Hey. Hey, lookit that dude!

TIM

Where?

DARRELL

Don't fucking stare . . . just casual. Ol' fucker in the *camouflage*. What a loser!

TIM

Prick—

DARRELL

I hate that crap! Vietnam assholes, still wear that fuckin' garb everywhere they go. *M.I.A.* T-shirts and shit.

TIM

That cock—

DARRELL

Catch this. (*loudly*) Hey man, you kill many *kids* when you were over there?
> (*They burst out laughing and flip off the middle-aged man.*)

Fuckin' retards . . . (BEAT) That wasn't a *war*, anyway, not like the Persian Gulf. My dad told me a bunch 'a shit they did over in Saudi . . . you wouldn't <u>believe</u> some 'a the stuff. He told me one time—just to make a point, he was there ten months or so, I think—and he said that, this is true, the <u>nicest</u> thing that happened when he was there, he was up in a helicopter and flying out to some base or somewhere, and they ran right into this flock of birds. Yeah, these, like, giant birds they got near *Kuwait* or some place like that, big fucking birds just migrating or who knows what, but they went ripping right through 'em at about a hundred fifty miles an hour . . . feathers, blood, all sorts 'a shit on everybody! He and around six or ten of the guys with him, just covered in bird guts! They barely landed the chopper thing, that's what he said. <u>And</u> they hardly get on the ground, at this outpost they're going to, and they get attacked by these fucking *ragheads*!—that's what they called the Iraqi guys, "ragheads"—really nasty shit, too, I guess, hand-to-hand stuff and they go into it already wearing all this crap on 'em! Big chunks of these, like, white birds . . . he said it really scared the fuck outta the Iraqis and they took off running. Seriously. I'm not shitting ya. He said they must've killed thirty or so of these birds and that was the *best* thing that happened while he was there. So, you can pretty much imagine the kind 'a fucking ordeal he went through. Not a holiday, anyway, some port on the *South China Sea*. (BEAT) Dad don't talk about it much, not when I see him, but he did tell me that he still feels bad about those birds. He told me that—

TIM

No shit?

DARRELL

Nope. (BEAT) Although I think he's making a big deal outta nothing. Bunch 'a *birds*, who gives a fuck?

TIM

Yeah.

DARRELL *shakes his head and the ice in his cup at the same time. He stands.*

DARRELL

You got any cash?

TIM

I just ate it.

DARRELL

Fuck. That won't do—

TIM *slides up the wall into a standing position.*

TIM

We waiting for Jenn or what?

DARRELL

She'll find us. Not a fucking cent, huh?

TIM

Uh-uh.

DARRELL

Well, we gotta remedy that. (BEAT) Stay out here, 'kay, I'm gonna pop back inside and look for her, maybe get a refill. See if I can get us a few bucks—

Before TIM *can answer* DARRELL *is gone.* TIM *is left alone, so he plops onto a bench and pulls a CD out of his pocket. He begins absently tearing at the wrapping.*

After a bit, JENN *appears. Seventeen, pretty, strong-featured. Uniform of the day (T-shirt, jeans) with a large bag over one shoulder. She stops cold when she sees* TIM.

JENN

—Tim. Oh. Hi.

TIM

Hey. 'S going on?

JENN

Nothing. You?

TIM

Just sittin'.

JENN

Oh. (BEAT) So, where's Darrell?

TIM

You know, around. Looking for you, I guess—

JENN

Huh. Which way'd he go?

TIM

He's gonna be right back. (BEAT) You can sit, if you wanna.

JENN

No.

TIM

'Kay.

JENN

See, I gotta . . . uhh, do you know which direction he went?

TIM

All over.

JENN

Fuck.

TIM

S'pposed to meet him here, right?

JENN

Talked about it, yeah, but, see, I need to go. I gotta go, and I don't want 'em all pissed off, so . . . anyway, I just gotta.

TIM

Oh.

TIM *nods then turns back to working on the CD wrapper.* JENN *stands there, uncomfortable.*

JENN

Tim.

TIM

Yeah?

JENN

How come you don't look at me when I say something anymore?

TIM

Huh?

JENN

A thing I noticed. Lately. I'm with you and Darrell, or just at a place, you're always looking away, off some other way. Not at me. How come?

TIM

—whatever. (BEAT) So, you're not staying?

JENN

Ummm—

TIM

'S all right.

JENN

See, I told some friends, I mean, you know—Shit!

JENN *looks around for a moment, then sits on the edge of the bench.* TIM *scoots down. After a moment, he holds out the CD.*

TIM

You like The Cult at all?

JENN

Uh-huh.

TIM

Here.

JENN

What?

TIM

Here. 'S yours.

JENN

No, I'm not gonna take—

TIM

Darrell swiped it. Gave it to me. No big deal—

JENN

Thanks.

TIM

Worry about it.

JENN

So . . . I'm gonna go, then. See you guys tomorrow, or—

TIM

Uh-huh.

She looks over at TIM, *then gives his hand a quick squeeze. He looks up at her.*

JENN

Do me a favor, 'kay? Don't say anything, I mean, like, that you saw me or whatnot. 'S probably better—

TIM

Right. Got it.

JENN

Okay, then. See ya . . .
(*She gets up and starts off, but turns back at the last moment.*)
'S that a new shirt?

TIM

No. My sister got it for me—

JENN

It's nice.

With that JENN *is gone, hurrying away toward the crossroads of the mall.* TIM *sits alone now in silence, examining his shirt.*

THE LIVING ROOM

Same as before, but with trays set up for dinner. The TV is blaring a game show. CAMMIE, RICH *and* DARRELL *take up the two chairs and sofa, hunched over their respective meals.*

RICH

—fucking salmon loaf, huh?

DARRELL

Yeah.

CAMMIE

Hey, don't start, okay, 'cause I'm gonna throw my plate at both 'a you, keep ripping this stuff to shreds.

RICH

What?

CAMMIE

Tastes like shit, I can't help it. I still gotta cook it, takes time to *prepare* it, doesn't it?

DARRELL

I'm not saying nothing.

RICH

Well, I am—(BEAT) Tastes like some thing. Something bad.
Fish. I hate that—

CAMMIE *looks at him but says nothing.* DARRELL *glances over, smiling.*

DARRELL

The fuck you think *salmon* is, Rich?

RICH

Should I know? Fucking gourmet chef, some TV show? I'm
saying what it tastes like, not what it is.

DARRELL

Oh man . . . listen, you gotta be kidding me, right? "Salmon."
He's just giving me shit, isn't he, Mom?

CAMMIE

I dunno.

RICH

I'll give you shit, pal, piece 'a this salmon loaf, 'ever the fuck
it is, all over your Zeppelin shirt.

CAMMIE *(barely amused)*

You two're like a couple brats over at nursery school. Drive me
nuts I gotta work there all day, come home find my *babies*
going at it. Knock it off and eat.
> (DARRELL *makes a face and* RICH *smiles. He*
> *throws a piece of his dinner at* DARRELL, *who*
> *ducks.*)
Hey, I said enough!

RICH *reaches over from his chair and pulls her close. She gives in and they*
kiss deeply while DARRELL *slips part of his salmon onto* RICH's *plate.*

DARRELL

Careful there, Rich, fucking tongue 'a hers'll be snaking down
your throat—

CAMMIE *glares at* DARRELL *and they all eat in silence for a few moments.*

RICH *(to* DARRELL*)*

Hey, you wanna go to the track with me, Friday night?

DARRELL

What's going on?

RICH

I need a *date*—

DARRELL

Figures.

RICH *punches* DARRELL *and they wrestle from where they're sitting.*

RICH

Stock cars're coming in, two weeks only. Got tickets from work.

DARRELL

That's cool.

CAMMIE

We're going tomorrow night, but thought you'd wanna go with Rich alone. Check out the "babes—"

RICH

No shit.
      (*She punches* RICH *on the arm.*)
Oww!!

CAMMIE

Be nice, two of you get out and do something. Right?

DARRELL

Yeah. Can Tim go with us?

RICH

Sure. Gotta pay full admit, though. Only two discounts per night. Per person.

DARRELL

No prob'. His mom's good for cash. Hint, hint—

CAMMIE

Uh-uh, I don't give a shit, I *earn* my money. You wanna buy hot dogs, sneak a beer, you need to round up your own, Sweetie—

DARRELL

Just kiddin' ya.

RICH

Maybe we can slip 'em in, trunk or some deal 'til we get inside the gates. Save us a couple bucks we'll get a pizza—

DARRELL

Cool. (BEAT) You get enough air, closed up space like that?

RICH

Fuck yeah. Go for miles in there.

DARRELL

Yeah?

RICH

No problem at all. What do you think, Cammie?

CAMMIE

Long as his Mom knows—

DARRELL

Great! No, that'd be *really* great. (BEAT) Shari going, or she
gonna hit the Thursday show with you guys?

CAMMIE

Nah, she can't get a sitter.

RICH

Can't *afford* it.

CAMMIE

Rich.

DARRELL

Oh.
>   (*Silence settles over them as* DARRELL *picks at his*
>   *food.* RICH *and* CAMMIE *exchange looks.*)
So, Rich, how's the car? Don't trust those fuckers down the
shop.

RICH

Still got a lotta trannie fluid dripping. I'm gonna take it back
over, maybe Monday, give 'em hell—

DARRELL

Yeah?

RICH

Fuck yes. Get to the *bottom* 'a this.

DARRELL

Oh. (BEAT) So, then, where's the . . .?

CAMMIE

It's in the garage. And don't even <u>think</u> about it.

A moment passes.

RICH

Hey, Babe, you get me a beer?

CAMMIE

Shit . . . you're a real *bargain*, you know?

RICH

Better believe it.
>   *They kiss again, then* CAMMIE *stretches and smiles,*
>   *tossing a look at* DARRELL *as she goes.*
She's a great woman. You know that, right?

DARRELL

What<u>ever</u>, man.

RICH *nods and stands, moving his tray out of the way and crossing to the door.*
He swings it open and fires up a smoke, holding his Lucky Strike outside.

RICH

So how's school?

DARRELL

Fucked.

RICH

Yeah. (BEAT) I went there, you knew that, right?

DARRELL

Uh-huh.

RICH

That ol' bitch in the office still there? Miss Pinch-Ass, something, her name—

DARRELL

Dickers? Kinda orange hair—

RICH

Shit yes! Fucking Dickers! That's her . . . What a cunt.

DARRELL

Oh yeah.

They share a brief smile as DARRELL *bums a cigarette.*

RICH

Blow it out here . . . hate the smell, love the fucking taste. What can I tell ya?

DARRELL

Right.

RICH

—hey, piece of advice?

DARRELL

Mmm?

RICH

Giving you a clue, pal . . . get the fuck outta here, you got the chance.

DARRELL

Huh?

RICH

Your step-sister's coming over. Bringing her fucking kid, gonna watch some kinda bullshit tape she bought. Sorry I ever lugged that fucking machine home now, know what I mean?

DARRELL

No shit. And bringing the baby?

RICH

Fuck else she gonna do with it?

DARRELL

Oh man—

RICH

Love to *punt* that little fucker into the next county! Crying his ass off all night, stinking up the place. Can't take that shit, day of humping fifty pounders 'a dog chow all over hell—

DARRELL

Yeah, I'm with ya.

They each take a drag, then RICH *looks back inside.*

RICH (*to* CAMMIE)

Honey, the fuck you doing, *brewing* the shit youself?!

DARRELL *laughs and* RICH *winks at him.*

DARRELL

Listen, I'm gonna take off. That kid hits me with a rattle or something, liable to fling 'em out the fucking window.

RICH

I'll hold it open for ya, buddy, believe me!

DARRELL *gives him a sympathy pat on the shoulder as* RICH *fakes a jab at him. They spar for a moment, which turns quickly into wrestling.* DARRELL *loses.*

DARRELL

Hey, come on! You fucking want me!! You like me, don't ya, you do—

RICH

Little prick, come on! Get off!! You are a squirrelly mother-fucker—

RICH *sits on top of him now, twisting his arm.*

DARRELL

'Kay, oww, shit, I give!!

RICH *laughs and pulls* DARRELL *to his feet. They slap at each other and then* DARRELL *grabs his coat.*

RICH

The fuck outta here . . .
> (DARRELL *smiles and disappears out into the night.* RICH *looks around as he lights up again. After a moment,* CAMMIE *appears with two beers.*)

Hey.

CAMMIE

Hi. (BEAT) Where'd Darrell go?

RICH

I dunno, took off. He's *your* kid. (BEAT) Why'd you take so long?

CAMMIE

Called my daughter—

RICH

<u>Step</u>. Step-daughter.

CAMMIE

You know what I mean. Told her to come in an hour. Give us some time to clean up . . . (BEAT) Did you tell Darrell they were coming?

RICH

Nah.

CAMMIE

'Cause he likes playing with the baby.

RICH

Hmmm. Maybe he went to get smokes or something, not sure.

CAMMIE *nods and leans back into* RICH's *arms; he offers her a drag on his cig. She takes it and closes her eyes.*

CAMMIE

—nice.

RICH

Tired?

CAMMIE

A little.

RICH

You wanna lay down or whatever . . . I can do up the dishes.
> (CAMMIE *laughs softly at the thought of this.* RICH
> *smiles.*)

Fuck you . . . I could.

CAMMIE

That's okay. Just gonna rest a second . . . You gotta say "screw this" every once in awhile, you know, and kick back. You do.

RICH

Yep.

RICH *kisses the top of her head. She responds and turns to him as they begin to kiss passionately in the open doorway.*

CAMMIE

Mmmmmmm . . . hey, you tell 'em his dad called?

RICH

Yeah, I mentioned it, yeah.

CAMMIE

You did?

RICH

Uh-huh . . . said he'd call him later.

CAMMIE

'Kay. (BEAT) Think he wants Darrell to come down and stay with 'em again this summer. Like he did two years ago—

RICH

Fine with me.

CAMMIE

Yeah, I don't care. Whatever.

RICH

Exactly.

CAMMIE *nods, then goes back to kissing* RICH. *They slide up roughly against the jam and continue.*

THE SCHOOL PARKING LOT

Endless square of asphalt, sectioned off by yellow lines. Sodium lights buzz overhead. A FACULTY PARKING ONLY *sign bolted to the pole. Empty this time of night.*

DARRELL *stands sharing a cigarette with two* TEENAGERS.

DARRELL

—fucking frigid, huh?

BOY

Yeah.

DARRELL

I mean, this time 'a year—

BOY

'S true.

DARRELL

Wind's roaring down from fucking Canada, freeze our dicks off 'cause of some shitty *jet stream*, something 'a that nature.

GIRL

Uh-huh. (BEAT) Where's Tim?

DARRELL

Fuck should I know?

GIRL

I dunno.

DARRELL

Probably work, hanging out with his gook buddies, whatever—

GIRL

Oh.

They shuffle about for a moment, puffing away on the cig.

DARRELL

Anybody got some cash? (BEAT) Come on, I got us that bottle
'a vodka! Fucker took *three* joints to give it to me—

BOY

I hate that guy . . . son-of-a-bitch's always working.

DARRELL

Nobody's got a fucking *dime*?

GIRL

I left my purse at home—

DARRELL

Great. (BEAT) Should go back and slash that motherfucker's
tires! That was fuckin' uncalled for . . . (*to the* BOY) Huh? You
wanna?

BOY

Uhhh . . . nah. Too far, man, walk all the way back there.

DARRELL

Seriously, though—

BOY

Get 'em next time.

DARRELL

Fuck—

GIRL

I don't care. If you feel like it, I'll walk back with you.

DARRELL *studies her a moment, then stubs out his smoke and lights another.*

DARRELL

Shit! Forget it . . . fucking frozen out here. I may head out, time is it?

BOY

Two-thirty. I should prob'ly take off.

DARRELL

'Kay. See ya.

BOY

Take it easy, man.

DARRELL

Yeah.

BOY

Bye.

GIRL

See you later, Darrell—

DARRELL

So long. (BEAT) Hey, you see Jenn today?

BOY

Nah, I think she was sick or something. Went home early.

GIRL

No, I saw her. At the mall. Having fries with that red-haired chick.

DARRELL

The one cute one?

GIRL

Yeah, Liz-whatever, and somebody else. Girl I don't know.

DARRELL

Huh.

GIRL

Uh-huh. Looked like her, anyway . . . over at the Big Boy's.

DARRELL

Oh. (BEAT) 'Kay. See ya.

GIRL

—I thought you guys broke up.

DARRELL

What, <u>no</u>. Told you that?

GIRL

I just, I dunno, heard it or whatever.

DARRELL

No way—

GIRL

Well, maybe I got it wrong. Maybe.

BOY

Fuck's that mean, all cryptic and shit?

DARRELL

You heard it or not. Which?

GIRL

—I thought I did.

DARRELL

Where?

GIRL

I dunno, just around.

DARRELL

Come on, no . . . that's, like, fucked.

GIRL

Oh.

DARRELL

Totally.
    (DARRELL *puts a stop to this by turning away and
    kicking at the blacktop.*)
So, she was with that red-haired girl?

GIRL

Think it was her—

DARRELL

A <u>girl</u>, though, right?

GIRL

Looked like it.

BOY

"Looked like" or not?

GIRL

I'm pretty sure, yes. That Liz. And this other one. (BEAT) Oh, and Tim, too.

DARRELL

Whaa?

GIRL

Outside, when I was first going in . . . I saw 'em talking for a minute.

DARRELL *(caught offguard)*

Oh. <u>Outside</u>. Whatever. I don't care—

GIRL

—right.

They stare at one another, then the BOY *waves and starts off.*

BOY

So, I'm outta here . . . see ya, dude.

DARRELL

Right.

BOY

You going tomorrow?

DARRELL

Later. Maybe some dodge ball in gym or something—

BOY

That'd be sweet! *(to the* GIRL*)* You coming?

She falters a moment, looking at DARRELL.

GIRL

Ummm, yeah, in a minute or so. Gonna bum a smoke first—

BOY

'Kay. Whatever—

He moves off into the darkness. DARRELL *stands with the girl in silence for a bit.*

DARRELL

—fucking weeknights, huh?

GIRL

Yeah.

DARRELL

Boring as shit—

GIRL

Yep.

DARRELL

That dick . . . wouldn't go back with me, cut those tires. I <u>knew</u> it!

GIRL

Nope.

DARRELL

'S like, hey, how 'bout a little support or whatever . . . meant to be *friends* here.

GIRL

I s'ppose.

DARRELL

Fuck's that supposed to mean?

GIRL

Just saying . . . (BEAT) Don't ever really *know* a person, right? Can't, not inside.

DARRELL

What?

GIRL

—nothing.

DARRELL

No, what? Hanging back, all secretive and shit tonight, don't think I caught that?

GIRL

Uh-uh—

DARRELL

Bullshit, "uh-uh," come with that guy and now standing around here, shooting it with me. What's up?

GIRL

No, I'm not doing anything, I just—

DARRELL

Five minutes and you ain't even *glanced* at my smoke, so don't fuck around. <u>What?</u>
     (*The* GIRL *shifts from one foot to the other, uneasy.*)
Go ahead . . . (*offers a puff*) Here.

He hands over the last of his Camel and she sucks it down.

GIRL

Listen—

DARRELL

Uh-huh?

GIRL

Jenn'd hate me if I told ya this—

DARRELL

So, why do it?

GIRL

'Cause. (BEAT) . . . I like you.

DARRELL

Yeah.

GIRL

You could tell?

DARRELL

Sorta. Always looking at me and shit.

GIRL

I know. (BEAT) So . . . maybe I shouldn't—

DARRELL

Start that "girl" crap, come on! Just say it.

GIRL

'S about Jenn. I mean, about Jenn and someone—

DARRELL

Uh-huh. Anybody I know?

GIRL

Ummm . . . I don't know the *whole* thing, I just . . . you know—

DARRELL

Fuck, just go for it.

GIRL

I only heard parts of it, from this guy I know. We're sorta re-lated. Works at the pet store—

DARRELL

Yeah, and?

GIRL

Listen . . . do you like me at all?

DARRELL

You're okay, yeah.

GIRL

Good. Great . . . cool.

DARRELL

'S absolutely fantastic. You're not careful, I'm gonna ask you to fucking *homecoming* . . . (*smiles*) Now, come on . . . who?

GIRL

—just . . . somebody.

THE LIVING ROOM

Same as before, but dinner has been cleared. Pushed aside, at least. Blankets on the couch. TV turned on.

SHARI *sits in a V-neck tee and undies, watching the tube.* DARRELL *just kicking off his shoes.*

DARRELL

—fucking early, huh?

SHARI

Yeah.

DARRELL

Still here, though.

SHARI

Uh-huh. Car wouldn't start. Rich said he'd look at it in the morning.

DARRELL

Great.

SHARI

—the, uhh, baby's in your bed. Hope you don't mind.

DARRELL

Nah.

SHARI

Your mom said it'd be okay.

DARRELL

Yeah. Sleep on the couch or whatever.
(*He moves toward the sofa and looks down at*
SHARI, *who just slides a bit down to make room.*)
'S that a problem?

SHARI

Well . . . umm, shit.

DARRELL

What?

SHARI

Cammie said I should sleep out here, you know, give the baby
some space. He's been kinda sick.

DARRELL

Oh.

SHARI

And they gotta work tomorrow.

DARRELL

Right.

SHARI

Yeah.

DARRELL

—umm, no, I'll take a couple cushions, sleep in the kitchen.

SHARI

No, you don't have to—

DARRELL

Fuck it, it's *sleep*, right? All the same to me.

SHARI

Thanks.

DARRELL

'S all right.

SHARI

That's sweet, Darrell, thanks.

DARRELL

No prob'. I'll just take 'em off the back there, okay? Leave you the bottom—

SHARI

I appreciate it. Don't really wanna be in there with the baby, he puked up earlier.

DARRELL

Yeah, I can *smell* it—

SHARI

Sorry.

DARRELL

Don't matter. I'll be in the <u>kitchen</u> . . . smells worse in there!

SHARI *laughs lightly as* DARRELL *smiles at her.*

SHARI

Have fun tonight?

DARRELL

'S all right. Saw some guys I know, shit like that.

SHARI

Nice.

DARRELL

Yep. 'Kay, good night—

He almost makes it to the door but SHARI *speaks again.*

SHARI

Darrell?

DARRELL

Yeah?

SHARI

I ever tell you . . . that I always liked you?

DARRELL

No.

SHARI

I mean, as kids. When we were all living together. Right after they got married.

DARRELL

Really?

SHARI

Yep, I always did. Thought you were really cute and everything, but, you know, brother and sister and all.

DARRELL

<u>Step</u>.

SHARI

True, but, I mean, supposed to be like it. Brother and sister.
They wanted us to *pretend* like we were, right?

DARRELL

I guess.

SHARI

Anyway. I liked you. You were funny and kinda nice so I just
liked you.

DARRELL

Huh.

Silence as SHARI *slowly undresses in front of* SHARI. *Shirt and pants.*
He stands now in his briefs, looking at her.

SHARI

I told you that before, though, right?

DARRELL

No. You never did.

SHARI

Oh. Well . . . (BEAT) Come 'ere a second.

SHARI *motions and* DARRELL *sits. The baby begins to cry.*

DARRELL

What?

SHARI

You're filling out, huh?

DARRELL

Little.

SHARI

No, you definitely are. Definitely.

DARRELL

We do weights at school sometimes . . . Univesal Gym or
whatnot.

SHARI

Looks good. Grown up—

DARRELL

Whatever.

SHARI

Look . . . you don't have to sleep out there, on the *linoleum*.
'Cause this pulls out to, like, you know, a Queen.

DARRELL

What, sleep here? Umm—

SHARI

Yes. We could just set it up and—

DARRELL

—nah, I should just—

SHARI

I'm gonna be running back and forth all night, anyway.

DARRELL

Yeah?

SHARI

I mean, listen to 'em! Fuck—

DARRELL

I guess.

SHARI

Just a lot more cozy, that's all I'm saying.

DARRELL

True.

SHARI

Be like when we were younger, times we'd do blanket forts
and shit. We can pretend it's like one 'a those—

DARRELL

Oh, man, come on!

SHARI

Seriously.

DARRELL

That's funny, I remember that—

SHARI

With that big flowered comforter out on the porch, 'member?
And the dog, that little spaniel thing would come tearing in there
and knocking shit over, stepping on our sandwiches and all—

DARRELL

Yeah. (*laughs*) That was funny—

CAMMIE *appears from a hallway, yawning and a bit cross. Long T-shirt
on with a tear in it near the belly.*

CAMMIE

—fucking crying, huh?

SHARI

Yeah.

CAMMIE

Think you can maybe . . .?

SHARI

Just gonna. Go back in, sorry.

CAMMIE

Coming right through the wall, you know.

SHARI

I'll get 'em, you guys sleep.

CAMMIE *nods and lights up a smoke. Inhales deeply then looks over at*
DARRELL, *who quickly stands.*

CAMMIE

Hey. Fuck you still up for?

DARRELL

Just got in.

CAMMIE

Oh. Didn't know. I mean, standing in your *undies* there—

DARRELL

Yeah, gonna hit the sack.

SHARI

We were just talking and stuff.

CAMMIE

'Bout what?

SHARI

You know, when we were kids. Shit like that.

CAMMIE

Uh-huh.

SHARI

When we played together, over in that one house, downtown?

CAMMIE

I remember.

DARRELL

We made a tent on the porch. Shari was telling me about it.

CAMMIE

On the porch?

DARRELL

With that flowered throw 'a yours, the big scratchy one off your bed.

CAMMIE

—I don't recall that. *Flowered*? No—

DARRELL

We did it, though, a couple times.

SHARI

On the <u>back</u> porch.

CAMMIE

Hmmm. I dunno . . . maybe I was at work or something.

DARRELL

Whatever. No big deal.

CAMMIE *takes another puff, motions to* SHARI *about the crying.*

SHARI

I'm going. (BEAT) Hey, Cammie, I was thinking that Darrell could maybe—

CAMMIE

You're set in the kitchen, right?

DARRELL

Ummm—

CAMMIE

You got the cushions there, so—

DARRELL

—'s fine. Yep.

CAMMIE

Great.

DARRELL

Whatever.

CAMMIE

Good, get going, then. And don't eat everything, neither. Leave some milk.

DARRELL

'Kay. (BEAT) I was just gonna have some more 'a that *salmon*, if it's all right—

CAMMIE

Smart ass.

She goes off to bed. SHARI *and* DARRELL *look at one another.*

SHARI

You can sneak back out later, I mean, if you want.

DARRELL

I'll think about it—

SHARI

Good. 'S a <u>Queen</u>-size, so you know—

DARRELL

Yeah. 'Night.

SHARI

'Night.

DARRELL *wanders off with his cushions. The baby cries.*

THE EMPTY LOT

Big slab of blacktop forced up against the back corner of a building. Several ash cans around. A place near school where kids gather to smoke. Empty now.

DARRELL *and* TIM *stand nearby with cigs, puffing away in silence.* DARRELL *yawns.*

DARRELL

—fucking bell, huh?

TIM

Yeah.

DARRELL

'Nother couple minutes, sitting in fucking science! *Double helix* can just lick me, ya know?

TIM

Right. You do the homework?

DARRELL

Tim, <u>think</u> about what you just said—

TIM

Oh.

DARRELL

You?

TIM

Yeah, my sister helped me out—

TIM *pulls a wrinkled page out of his textbook as evidence.* DARRELL *nods.*

DARRELL

Cool. (BEAT) Can I copy it?

TIM

Sure. I'm not, like, for *certain* that it's right or nothing.

DARRELL

Gives a shit?

TIM

That's what I figured. Something to have 'case she calls on me—

DARRELL

Absolutely.

DARRELL grabs TIM's *homework from his hand, pushing* TIM *away when he tries to get it back. Studying it,* DARRELL *snags one of* TIM's *notebooks off the pavement and starts to scribble down figures.*

TIM

Change a coupla answers, though, make it too obvious—

DARRELL

Way ahead of you, dude.

TIM

'Kay.

DARRELL

Always way the fuck out there in front 'a you, Timmie.

TIM

Don't call me that, man.

DARRELL

Whatever. Just want you to know that I'm on to you, 'ever you try and pull that *covert* shit 'a yours.

TIM

What?

DARRELL

"What?" you know fuckin' what.

TIM

—no.

DARRELL

Yesterday. (BEAT) The mall.

TIM

I dunno, what? Serious.

DARRELL

Fuck you, lie right to my face.

TIM

Darrell, <u>what?</u>

DARRELL

Ahh, Jenn, maybe. You fucking saw her, I know you did.

TIM

I did not . . . (BEAT) . . . She say something?

DARRELL

Nice fucking pal I got.

TIM

Hey . . . she asked me not to. The hell am I gonna do?

DARRELL

Ummm, maybe not be a total butthole and keep shit from me.
(BEAT) I *hate* that, more than any thing on this fucking earth.
Lies and such.

TIM

—sorry. Put me in a bind.

DARRELL

Yeah, well, don't do that shit again. I mean it—

TIM

'Kay.

DARRELL *punches* TIM *on the arm, hard, and* TIM *takes it. They share an uneasy smile.*

DARRELL

Listen . . . you got, like, twenty bucks or whatnot I can borrow?
Gotta get Jenn a present, perfume 'a some kind. Something.
Birthday's tomorrow—

TIM

Nah. Really?

DARRELL

Yeah. (BEAT) Nothing?

TIM

Uh-uh. Mom cut off my fucking allowance . . . I spray painted
some shit in the family room. Sorry.

DARRELL

Great. (BEAT) What about work, they do pay you, right, or you
just like hanging out with those chop suey motherfuckers?

TIM

I get, like, a check next week—

DARRELL

Too late! Birthday's on *Friday*. (BEAT) Fuck!

TIM *doesn't answer and* DARRELL *impatiently waves him off, going back to copying the work.* TIM *begins to examine his jeans. Tries to lighten things up.*

TIM

Look—

DARRELL

What?

TIM

—found a coupla welts on my legs, showering this morning. Fucking ants!

DARRELL

Uh-oh, lemme feel your head—

DARRELL *starts to wrestle with* TIM, *trying to get a hand on his forehead.*

TIM

Knock it off, faggot! You fucker!! <u>Don't</u> call me that!!!

DARRELL

Hey, come on! I can feel it, Timmie, you're going bonkers!! Whoooah!!!

The fighting increases until DARRELL *connects with a hard slap to* TIM'S *face. Suddenly the game is serious.* DARRELL *goes at* TIM *again, who hits him with a solid shot to the chest.* DARRELL *staggers back from the blow.*

TIM

Shit, sorry!

DARRELL

Dick!!

TIM

Well—

DARRELL

Use a fucking fist! I was just *playing*, you prick . . . (BEAT) That's illegal in wrestling, you know, closed hand?!

TIM *nods at this, solemnly accepting the rebuke.* DARRELL *uses the opportunity to jump* TIM *and bring him to the ground. They battle each other as* JENN *enters.*

JENN

—hey.

DARRELL

Shit. (BEAT) Hi, Jenn, what's up?

JENN

Nothing. Figured you guys'd be here . . . didn't know you'd be *making* out.
> (DARRELL *laughs this off and quickly stands, brushing himself off.* TIM *remains where he is, then rises slowly.*)

Hey, Tim.

TIM

Jenn. How you doing?

JENN

You know.

TIM

Yeah.

DARRELL

He sure does. He knows a fucking *ton* . . . 'course he never tells me. Like about yesterday, for instance.

JENN *fires a look directly at* TIM; DARRELL *catches it before she turns back.*

JENN

—what?

TIM

Darrell . . . (*to* JENN) I didn't say shit—

DARRELL

Nah, don't worry, Jenn, he lied his ass off for ya.

JENN

Whatever.

DARRELL

Yeah, which I don't understand, since he says he dislikes ya so much . . . (BEAT) Hey, did you call Tim "stupid" or something?

JENN

What?!

TIM

Aww, fuck!

TIM *quickly gathers his books and starts to move away.*

DARRELL

Tim, I'm kidding! Get over here!!

TIM

I gotta take a pee. See ya in class—

JENN

'Bye, Tim. Still got detention later?

TIM

See ya, Jenn. Yeah. Uh-huh.

DARRELL *waves and* TIM *walks off.* JENN *turns back to* DARRELL.

JENN

Fuck you gotta be so shitty for, huh?

DARRELL

Hey, you're the one who said it.

JENN

God! Talking at some party last month, drunk as hell . . . can't you just be nice? Your own fucking *friend.* You know?

DARRELL

Whatever. (BEAT) The fuck you do that for yesterday? Blow me off—

JENN

Dunno.

DARRELL

I'm asking so I'm interested. (BEAT) Come on, I missed you.

JENN

—yeah? How much?

DARRELL

This much.

DARRELL *grabs the crotch of his jeans and makes a face.* JENN *laughs a bit, hits at him.*

JENN

So, I guess that says we're just, like, back together, huh? I mean, way you're acting suddenly—

DARRELL

What?

JENN

The hell was all that shit on Monday, "what?"

DARRELL

Nothing. I was pissed—

JENN

Yeah, I got that! (BEAT) The dude's in my *homeroom*, okay, asked me a question, not my fucking number. All right?

DARRELL

No, it's not *all right*, you know I hate that shit! Other guys and shit—

JENN

Wasn't about a guy! Je-sus—

DARRELL

Well, fuck I know what goes on being my back . . . everybody sneaking around.

JENN

A little trust, maybe. Try that.
        (*They stare at one another a moment.* JENN *lightens up first.*)
Fuck . . . whatever.

DARRELL

'S not.

JENN

Then stop with the . . . you know, not every guy around is try'na get in my pants.

DARRELL

—yeah. (*smiles*) Maybe.

JENN

You gotta ease back on the jealous shit a little, 'kay, 'cause I'm tired 'a breaking up, like, every *three* days.

DARRELL

Come on. Don't worry 'bout it. (*tries to hug her*) 'S okay if you wanna hang with friends—

JENN

Yeah, well, don't be such a dick about it, then . . . (BEAT) I don't know about you sometimes, I really don't. Fucking *green eyed monster*—

DARRELL

Okay, okay, 's my fault.
          (*Another bell rings loudly.*)
Fuck! We doing something this weekend?

JENN

I guess. Sure.

DARRELL

Got any money?

JENN

Couple bucks, that's it.

DARRELL

Shit.

JENN

Might get a little tomorrow. My, ahh, *birthday*—

DARRELL

Don't worry, I'm getting ya one, two things!

JENN

'S not what I meant!

DARRELL

Bullshit!! (*they kiss*) I'll call ya—

JENN

When?

DARRELL

Dunno.

JENN

You get the car?

DARRELL

Uh-huh. Think so—

JENN

Great, see ya later, then. (BEAT) Hey, can you pick me up some
cigs?

DARRELL

Yeah. Sure.

JENN

Thanks. Love ya—

She kisses him again and goes off. DARRELL, *alone now, continues to smoke.*

DARRELL

—whatever.

THE DETENTION CENTER

Big, empty space taken up by numerous desks and metal bookshelves. THINK POSITIVE! *poster over the drinking fountain. A teacher's desk and chair are located in the back of the room.*

TIM *and* JENN *sit in opposing seats, hanging out;* JENN *is drawing in her notebook and* TIM *stares up at the clock.*

TIM

—fucking . . . time, huh? Slow.

JENN

Yeah. (*laughs*) You sound like Darrell.

TIM

Oh. Not trying to . . . just 'cause we hang out, probably.

JENN

Right.

TIM

Whatever. I mean . . . (BEAT) I'm not getting you nothing for your birthday. Just thought I'd tell you.

JENN

Huh. Okay.

TIM

Not 'cause, I mean, anything. Just don't get paid 'til next week, so—

JENN

No biggie. You gave me that one CD.

TIM

Yeah, but that wasn't—

JENN

That's plenty. More than I'll get at home—

TIM

Right. (BEAT) Darrell's buying ya some stuff. Don't say nothing, though, 'cause—

JENN

I know. I won't.

TIM

Good. Thanks.

JENN

No problem.

TIM

Anyways, I'm not gonna have nothing for you . . . (BEAT) I
would, though, if I could. Maybe. Just a little thing.

JENN

Thanks, Tim.

TIM

Sure. What?

JENN *studies him, then rips a piece of paper out of her notebook. Hands
it and some colored pencils to* TIM.

JENN

Here. Make me a card . . .

TIM *looks at her, glances around the room, then hurridly takes the
materials.*

TIM

—'kay.
        (TIM *starts to draw something quickly, covering it
        with a hand so* JENN *can't see.* JENN *smiles at this,
        then goes back to her work. After a moment,* DAR-
        RELL *enters and sneaks up on* TIM. *He makes a
        sudden animal roar and grabs* TIM *around the
        waist.* JENN *and* DARRELL *laugh at this.*)
Awww, fucker! Stop!!

DARRELL *plops down into another desk. He tries to see what* JENN *is
working on but she pulls it away.* TIM *folds up his paper and jams it in a
coat pocket.* JENN *notices this.*

DARRELL

—fucking <u>hypothalamus</u>, huh?

TIM

Yeah.

DARRELL

What do I care my brain fucks around with my *metabolic process* . . . give two shits about it?

JENN

Uh-huh.

DARRELL

Come after and "clean the board." Fuck her! Right? Who's she think she is, anyway?

TIM

Dunno.

DARRELL

No shit, Tim, I know you "dunno." Fuck do you <u>know?</u> Certainly not the answer to number three!

TIM

Yeah, I told you I wasn't so—

DARRELL

God! Like to find her, edge of a park somewheres . . . trying to start her car, bad *distributor cap*, some shit like that . . . and just beat the <u>fuck</u> outta her, leave 'er for the grounds crew come morning! What I feel for that bitch—

JENN

Darrell, don't be so—

TIM

—kinda cute, I think. I mean, for a <u>teacher</u> and all.

DARRELL

I can't even talk to you two . . . like a fucking *separate* wavelength or something.

TIM

She is, though! Not more than twenty-five, looks like—

DARRELL

Shit! Any chance you're gonna listen to me, pick up on the

fuck I'm saying?! Didn't question the twat's look, some two-piece *French cut*! Not saying she wouldn't be a primo prom choice, you in a goddamn *cummerbund*! Said she annoyed me, like to fuck-her-up!! Making me an <u>ass</u>, front of everybody—

TIM

Yeah, you did look kinda *stupid* up there—
>   (TIM *and* JENN *giggle at this until* DARRELL *reacts*
>   *violently, slapping* TIM *hard on the head.*)

Oww, bastard!

DARRELL

Just watch it, man! Fuck you calling *"stupid—"*

JENN

Come on, Darrell!

TIM

Kidding around—

DARRELL

Watch your fucking <u>self</u>, that's all.
>   (*A momentary standoff.* TIM *blinks first, looking up*
>   *at the clock again.* DARRELL *smacks his hand down*
>   *loudly on the desk. He looks around.*)

—fucking *punitive*, huh?

JENN

Yeah.

DARRELL

That's what this is. Some kinda piece a shit <u>police action</u>.

JENN

It's okay.

DARRELL

No, it isn't! Detention is bullshit, and I don't buy into any of that, alright, so don't "it's okay" me, 'cause I feel you've been wronged. Fucking *flexing* their muscles—

JENN

Darrell, 's no big thing. (BEAT) You probably shouldn't be in here, though—

DARRELL

—and who gave it to you? Dickers, I s'ppose.

JENN

Uh-huh. Caught me in the bathroom yesterday. Lightin' up.

DARRELL

Yeah, taking her two o'clock dump. Like fucking *clockwork*, right?

TIM

Yep.

The three of them share a laugh.

DARRELL

Cunt.

JENN

Darrell—

DARRELL

What?

JENN

Don't.

DARRELL

Huh?

JENN

I hate that word.

DARRELL

'S what she is, though. Rich called her that, and she is—

JENN

Doesn't mean you have to say it.

DARRELL

No, it doesn't. Don't mean I can't, though—

JENN

Not around me, then, 'kay? (BEAT) 'S the kinda thing my Dad'd say, you know, say it and screaming and shit . . . so don't.

DARRELL

Whatever.

An uncomfortable moment passes. TIM *clear his throat as a bell rings in the distance.*

TIM

She's gonna be back—

DARRELL

Fuck. (*thinks about it*) Come on, Jenn, let's get outta here, go
do something—

JENN

What, I got 'til 3:30.

DARRELL

So? Let's bolt—

JENN

Nah.

DARRELL

Why?

JENN

'S my fifth. Kicked out if I don't take it—

DARRELL

Who cares?

JENN

Don't stay if you don't wanna.

TIM (*to* DARRELL)

I'll go—

DARRELL

I mean, shit . . . 's like *I'm* taking it, too, I hang out the library
or whatnot, waiting for you guys.

JENN

I know.

DARRELL

Right?

TIM

—go outside with ya and smoke or something, if you wanna.
'S an idea.

DARRELL

Hey, Mr. Ideas, why don't you go study up on your *periodic
tables*, shit 'a that nature, 'stead of dishing advice, okay?

DARRELL *kicks* TIM *in the leg then turns back to* JENN. TIM *plays with a
colored pencil.*

JENN

So . . . you gonna hang or not?

DARRELL

Ummm, nah. I mean, no sense dragging us all down—

JENN

Whatever.

DARRELL

That'd just be <u>stupid</u>. Right, Timmie?

DARRELL *looks at* TIM *for emphasis.* TIM *shakes his head and moves over to the door.*

JENN

Just gotta keep it going, don't ya?
> (DARRELL *nods and smiles, then moves over to the
> wooden desk. He tests the drawers and then forces
> one open. A snap! of wood.*)

Darrell—

TIM *(glancing outside)*

Come on, man . . . I think she's coming!

DARRELL

Hold it.
> (DARRELL *moves quickly through the compart-
> ment, rummaging and pocketing some change as
> he digs. He suddenly produces a half pack of ciga-
> rettes and tosses them to* JENN. *He closes the
> drawer and saunters back.*)

There's those smokes I promised you—

JENN

Great. That's great—

DARRELL

See ya.

He touches JENN's *face briefly, then exits.* TIM *hovers at the door for an uncomfortable moment.*

TIM

—'bye.

JENN

Yeah.

At the last second, TIM *moves back inside and hands* JENN *his folded up "card."*

TIM

Here's your . . . thing. I didn't get to finish, but, you know—

JENN

Thanks, Tim. Thanks a lot.

He starts to say something but heads for the door. At the last second, JENN *mimes for* TIM *to call her. He nods and disappears into the hall.*

JENN *sits back in her seat and quickly hides the package of smokes in her coat. After a moment, she opens the card and reads it. Reads it again. Her eyes well up with tears.*

THE LIVING ROOM

The same again, TV trays still out. Dishes on them. TV blasting with a rerun of Walker: Texas Ranger.

DARRELL *stands in the kitchen archway, eating a banana. He looks down at* RICH, *who lies on the couch, eyes closed.* RICH *is still wearing his work-pants but without a shirt.*

DARRELL

—fucking bed, huh?

RICH

Yeah.

DARRELL

You sleep in the thing, like, *twice,* and she's gotta strip it down, bleach the shit outta it.

RICH

Uh-huh. Works hard, though.

DARRELL

She does, yeah, you're right—

RICH (*looking up at this*)

Cammie back yet?

DARRELL

Nah. Getting us some KFC . . . 's always packed in there.

RICH

Oh. (BEAT) Anyway, don't mind resting out here, better'n a
bare mattress.

DARRELL

Yeah. (BEAT) . . . so, fuck, sorry about the tickets, Rich.

RICH

No big deal, We're seeing 'em tonight, anyway. Go with one 'a
the guys from work tomorrow, sell 'em if not . . . worry about
it. (BEAT) Tim still wanna go?

DARRELL

Ahh, I think he's gonna do the birthday thing with us.

RICH

Figured. Thought I'd ask.

DARRELL

I 'ppreciate it. Would've been <u>cool</u>—

RICH

Yep. Should be some good heats, sounds like. (BEAT) Your
mom says I should take Shari, get 'er away from the kid for a
couple hours . . . I dunno.

DARRELL

She gonna do with 'em, though? Dump 'em here, I s'pppose,
fucking Friday night?!

RICH

Cammie don't mind .'Nother night of *toddlers*, fuck's the dif-
ference, right?

DARRELL

I guess. Still sucks—

RICH

Yep, but I got the *tickets*, now.

DARRELL

Sorry. Fuck! I <u>am</u> sorry—

RICH

She wanna come with us? Her birthday, do a little cake some
restaurant if you wanna—

DARRELL

Umm, well, you know . . . doesn't *know* you.

RICH

Forget it. An idea.

DARRELL

Shit.

RICH

Work it out. Got 'em for thirty bucks, not like I'm out a *bundle* . . .

>   (RICH *lays his head back on the armrest, rubbing*
>   *his eyes.*)

I gonna relax now. Fucking headache, like the *Concorde* taking off 'side my skull—

DARRELL

'Kay.

DARRELL *doesn't move. After a moment,* RICH *looks up.*

RICH

Darrell, I'm laying down, alright? Nice chatting with ya—

DARRELL

Listen, Rich, you got any . . . ummmm, oh, fuck. (BEAT) Hey, you have a little money I could borrow?

RICH

Huh?

DARRELL

Need to get a present. Just a *tiny* sort 'a something—

RICH

You come in here for this?

DARRELL

No, I just—

RICH

'Cause that's shitty, engage in some conversation, you just need to *bilk* me, my paycheck. Scam like that—

DARRELL

I remembered, just now, swear to God! I was gonna—

RICH

Forget it.

DARRELL

I don't need it if it's—

RICH

Just yanking you around. I'm kidding . . . Check my wallet, over by the keys there.

RICH *sits up as* DARRELL *moves to a counter and looks through the billfold. As he does,* DARRELL *secretly pockets a set of car keys;* RICH *misses this.*

DARRELL

—nothing.

RICH

Shit. Sorry.

DARRELL *stands for a long minute, staring into the empty pockets. Finally, he closes it and tosses it to* RICH.

DARRELL

'S no prob'. Really.

RICH

Gotta check with your mom.

DARRELL *nods and starts to leave; he stops short, looking at the edge of* RICH's *hip that is exposed.*

DARRELL

The fuck's that?

RICH

What?

DARRELL

That! Side 'a your hip there—

RICH

This? (*looks for a moment*) Body count.

DARRELL

Huh?

RICH

Fucking Saddam & Co. I never showed you this?

DARRELL

No! Cool—

RICH

Yep. (BEAT) We'd get a mark—drink a little something, ever

the fuck we had on hand—one 'a your buddies'd make a quick
cut, edge 'a your ass for the day's kill. Lot 'a guys had 'em.

                        DARRELL
That is, like, fucking *neat*! Can I see?
            (RICH *rolls over slightly, exposing his side as he
            pulls his pants down a touch.*)
No way . . . thir<u>teen</u>?!

                        RICH
Right.

                        DARRELL
Holy shit—

                        RICH
And that's not villagers, any mistakes we made. All those are
confirmed kills. <u>Bona fide</u> sandniggers.

                        DARRELL
Man, my dad doesn't have any stuff like that! Maybe he was
in another part of the desert or something—

                        RICH
Not all the guys got these. And he was not in Airborne. Lot 'a
shit went down, you're in fucking <u>Airborne</u>—
            (DARRELL *marvels at this, sitting on the sofa for a
            moment.*)
Touch 'em if ya wanna—

                DARRELL (*running a finger along*)
Fuck . . . 's totally badass. Serious.

                        RICH
Yep.

                        DARRELL
You like it over there?

                        RICH
Like?

                        DARRELL
You know—

                        RICH
I dunno "like." What's to fucking like, guys shooting *rockets* at
your ass.

DARRELL

Right, but . . . they give you a fucking gun. That's pretty hot.

RICH

It was nice. Yeah, the gun <u>was</u> nice.

DARRELL

Thirteen. That's incredible—

RICH

Got two, my last day.

DARRELL

Wwoooahh!

RICH

—you know what I did <u>like</u>, though? I mean this, I liked one thing.

DARRELL

What?

RICH

The toys. (BEAT) I really got into the kinds 'a *toys* they make in that place—

DARRELL

Yeah?

RICH

I'm serious . . . crazy war, I know, but they really had some great gifts and shit, all over that country. (BEAT) R&R, I'm in Riyadh, two, a couple weeks before we're outta there, standing outside this store, little sorta mud-type joint, I'm talking to a girl. Maybe ten, eleven years old. Trying to get me in bed, her <u>and</u> her mother, imagine what I'm telling you! The pair for, maybe, *six* bucks. Everybody thinks they're, like, so *religious* and all that nonsense, but believe me, they pull some pretty incredible shit over there. Did with us anyhow . . . (BEAT) So, like I say, I'm heading off with her, right, this kid, heading out but I just stop in front of this place I'm talking about, I mean literally come to a dead halt the colors are, like, so fucking *overwhelming*! I give the girl a buck or so—more money she's seen, her entire life—say I'll be along in a minute, and I stand there and just gotta squint to take it all in. Really. (BEAT) Gadgets, novelties, these whirly things buzzing all over hell . . . handmade shit like you've never seen! I'm inside, haggling with some guy, a hundred years old or whatnot—crazy fucker, spoke not a word 'a English—but he takes me out in the street, gets me to put one of his newest kites up in the air . . . it was this beautiful birdlike thing, I never known anything like it. Huge white wings just all out, must've had a span of, maybe, twenty feet or so, I shit you not . . . long graceful neck and this head, if you could've seen the head! This is what I'm talking about, this *ingenious* little fuck had made, I don't know how, but the head was like almost a separate kite that opened up when you got the thing high enough . . . Christ, it was just *stunning*! I'm telling you, the likes of it I don't imagine to see again, I don't care I live forever, nothing will be as miraculous as that fucking kite.

DARRELL

Wow—

RICH

Yeah. I must've had it up there, oh, at least a good couple hundred feet . . . the ol' guy ran inside, screaming his ass off, chattering away and just <u>beaming</u> with pride. He got a huge spool 'a string and we tied it on near the end and we just kept going with it . . . up over the old part a' the city, you know, where they got all the mosques and shit, we were way above that! Me and that bastard, trading off, circle 'a people around . . . Goddamn. It was <u>something</u>, I gotta tell you . . . (BEAT) Anyway, bought a couple things to send to my brother—he was twelve then, he used to get into all that *exotic* shit—and that was a hell of a good time for an R&R. (BEAT) Never did find that girl and her mom, though—

They share a long silence.

DARRELL

'S pretty trippy. Really—

RICH

Yep.

DARRELL

Six bucks, huh? <u>Both</u> of 'em?

RICH

Something like that.

DARRELL

That's *wild*. (BEAT) I gotta go, but I'll see ya—

RICH

Yep. Sorry 'bout the cash.

DARRELL

Uh-huh. So long, Rich.

DARRELL *exits. Once he is gone,* RICH *reaches deep into a pant pocket, producing a wad of cash. He reaches for his wallet, slowly stuffing the bills into a side flap.*

RICH (*to himself*)

—fucking kite must've been up half a mile, I'll bet.

THE PET STORE

Walls of fish, cages of cats and dogs. Stacks of supplies. A bit dirty. A poster announces BABY CHIMP IN STORE SATURDAY!

DARRELL *and* TIM *stand near the puppy cage, looking in. An* EMPLOYEE *leans to one side, a broom in one hand.*

DARRELL

—fucking mongrels, huh?

TIM

Yeah.

DARRELL

Slobber all over ya, hump the leg 'a every guest you got at your house.

EMPLOYEE

Only the guy dogs—

DARRELL

Yeah, but who wants a *bitch*, right?
> *They all share a quick laugh.* TIM *checks* DARRELL's
> *watch.*

Thought 'a getting one for my girlfriend, it's her birthday.

EMPLOYEE

Good idea.

DARRELL

I thought so. (BEAT) Put me into a puppy for, like, what? Ten
bucks—

EMPLOYEE

Sounds reasonable. (BEAT) . . . so, you guys go to Washington,
right?

DARRELL

Uh-huh. Fucking Washington <u>High</u>.

TIM

Juniors.

EMPLOYEE

Cool. (BEAT) I used to hang with some guy went to Washington—

DARRELL

'S what I heard. That one chick—

EMPLOYEE

Right.

DARRELL

<u>Lucky</u> you. Place's full 'a dumbshits, most of 'em. *Stupid* fuck-
ing freaks.

DARRELL *looks at* TIM, *who turns and busies himself with a cat toy.*

EMPLOYEE

He was this black dude. Guy I know. Played ball for Washington—

DARRELL

Oh, wow, a black dude who played fucking "ball," huh? What
a *surprise*—

EMPLOYEE

Right! (*laughs*) Exactly.

DARRELL

—he also a pretty good dancer?

EMPLOYEE

No doubt! I do not doubt it—

TIM

Get into hip-hop at all?

EMPLOYEE

I bet he does—

DARRELL

Fuck them . . . <u>rhythm</u> out their fucking asses. Don't do 'em a speck 'a good.

EMPLOYEE

True.

DARRELL *looks around the store. Quiet tonight.* TIM *checks* DARRELL's *watch again.*

DARRELL

The fuck you doing?!

TIM

Nothing, just—

DARRELL

Wanna hold my hand, just *ask* me—

TIM

Faggot.

DARRELL

Hey, you're the one feeling me up!

TIM

Trying to see the—

DARRELL

'S quarter to. What's up?

TIM

Oh man, I better get going—

DARRELL

"Going?"

TIM

Yeah, I said already . . . gotta get over to work. 'Member? I'm supposed to help out tonight—

DARRELL

No. You never said that.

TIM

I did, too.

DARRELL

<u>Nope</u>, uh-uh. When?

EMPLOYEE

We're closing up in fifteen, so—

With that, the EMPLOYEE *begins to halfheartedly sweep up.*

DARRELL

Hold on a sec'. (*to* TIM) I don't recall you saying that—

TIM

Thursday night. We always, ahh, they like to rotate the vats with fresh—

DARRELL

Hey, don't get all *Einstein* on me . . . the fuck does that mean? "Vats?"

TIM

In the fryers. Big cooking things we got.

DARRELL

So?

TIM

Before the weekend they prefer to drop in all new oil . . . 's just routine.

DARRELL

Fussy little fuckers, ain't they?

TIM

Yeah. 'S, like, practically a *religion* or something with these guys—

DARRELL *stands there sizing* TIM *up, not sure he believes him.*

DARRELL

Huh. So, you want me to swing by later?

TIM

Ummm, you know . . . don't know how long I'm gonna—

DARRELL

After, then? Wanna call me or . . .?

TIM

Could. Sure, if you . . . (*yawns*) Kinda tired, though.

DARRELL

Hey, not your fucking *spouse*, okay, don't gotta make up stories to cover your ass. Just say "no."

TIM

No, I can hang later if . . . I just gotta work on that History thing. The timeline.

DARRELL *(laughing)*

Fuck, okay, Tim, I get it. See ya in the A.M.
        (TIM *nods and starts off, but he is stopped by*
        DARRELL.)
Tim?

TIM

Yeah?

DARRELL

—where's your uniform?

TIM

Huh?

DARRELL

That *polyester* piece 'a shit they force on you. I don't see it.

TIM

No, I—

DARRELL

I know it ain't a pride issue 'cause you wear the fucker to school sometimes, so . . . where is it?

TIM

I don't have it.

DARRELL

How come? I mean, since you're going to *work* and all.

TIM

—just 'cause.

DARRELL

Nice comeback. Where is it?

TIM

Home. Only doing street clothes tonight, 'cause I'm not out front at all.

DARRELL

Oh.

TIM

Serious.

DARRELL

Fine. (BEAT) And you wouldn't be just, like, *ditching* me or anything? Right?

TIM

No. Fuck no, I mean—

DARRELL

So, I mean, if I swing past there later, just a check-in, you can toss me some *eggrolls* out the back door, no problem. Right?

TIM

—yeah.

DARRELL

Good, then. So get the fuck gone.

TIM

See ya. (BEAT) Hope you find something good, for, you know—

DARRELL

Yeah. I know.

TIM

Later.

DARRELL

Whatever.

> TIM *exits off into the mall.* DARRELL *watches him go, checking his watch. The* EMPLOYEE *makes his way back to the counter.*

Okay I smoke in here?

EMPLOYEE (*looking around*)

—yeah, just open the back door there.

DARRELL

Thanks. (*firing up*) So, who's this guy, anyway, dude you know. What's the big deal?

EMPLOYEE

No biggie—

DARRELL

Yeah?

EMPLOYEE

Nope.

DARRELL

So how come that one chick sent me over here to see ya? What's up?

EMPLOYEE

Nothing. Her idea.

DARRELL

Oh.

EMPLOYEE

She's my cousin. Sorta.

DARRELL

Yeah?

EMPLOYEE

Uh-huh. (BEAT) Pretty cute for a *cousin*, right?

DARRELL

Pretty fucking cute for <u>anybody</u>.

EMPLOYEE

Exactly. Said I should talk to you.

DARRELL

Yeah, but . . . <u>why</u>?

EMPLOYEE

A girl. Girl I saw in here the other day, I was having lunch with my cousin. Before work.

DARRELL

Yeah, and?

EMPLOYEE

Nothing. I just saw her. (BEAT) I got transferred over to this store 'bout five weeks ago, so—

DARRELL

Fucking *fascinating*—

EMPLOYEE

Anyhow, 's your girlfriend, I guess.

DARRELL

Oh.

EMPLOYEE

My cousin spotted her, said they went to school together, and I recognized her.

DARRELL

<u>You</u> know Jenn?

EMPLOYEE

Yeah. I mean . . . not "know" her, but you know. Seen her before. Sorta.

DARRELL

Huh. From where?

EMPLOYEE

This guy, guy I was talking about just now. The ballplayer. Through him.

DARRELL

—really?

EMPLOYEE

Yeah, he was with her. Well, not "with," but—

DARRELL

<u>What?</u> When was this?

EMPLOYEE

Ummm, I dunno . . . the summer before last, maybe. Yeah. 'Bout then.

DARRELL (*thinking it through*)

'Kay. (BEAT) . . . huh.

EMPLOYEE

We were hanging out, him and me, and so I'd see him at parties and shit—

DARRELL

Right, right. And?

EMPLOYEE

Hey . . . you sure you wanna hear all this shit? I mean, she said you would, my cousin did, but you seem—

DARRELL

No, fuck yeah, not a problem.

EMPLOYEE

You sure?

DARRELL

Absolutely. Totally. If it's about her, I mean—

EMPLOYEE

It is, yeah, definitely is.

DARRELL

Then cool. (BEAT) 'S before we were dating, anyway, so, just curious—

EMPLOYEE

Oh. (BEAT) Really? That's . . . I thought my cousin said you guys had been going out for—

DARRELL (*trying to bluff*)

Nah, what, two summers ago? That was, no, I was at my Dad's, so <u>way</u> before we ever hooked up. Definitely.

EMPLOYEE

Huh. Well, whatever. (BEAT) Anyway—

DARRELL

Yeah, so, what else? I mean—

EMPLOYEE

I'd see him around, like I said. Downtown and at his place. No big thing.

DARRELL

Cool.

EMPLOYEE

—'cept for the videos. (*laughs*) Those were a little different.

DARRELL

You lost me.

EMPLOYEE

Tapes that this guy made, down his basement. Of girls 'n him. You know, doing shit—

DARRELL

"Tapes."

EMPLOYEE

Yeah, he had this whole camera thing he'd rigged up—shit he stole, got from his dad, whatever it was—he fuckin' films chicks all the time, this hole in the *paneling*. And she was one of 'em.

DARRELL

—what?

EMPLOYEE

Yeah. Took me a sec' to realize it was her, but sure of it. Once I saw the face.

DARRELL

Huh.

EMPLOYEE

Yep.

DARRELL

—and, you, like, saw them? The videos, I mean.

EMPLOYEE

No, not all the time or anything, but every so often he'd pop one in—

DARRELL

Well, well—

EMPLOYEE

Pretty fucking hot—

DARRELL

Wow. So, doing stuff and whatnot?

EMPLOYEE

Yep.

DARRELL

—like?

EMPLOYEE

Just regular things. Mostly.

DARRELL

"Mostly?" 'S that mean?

EMPLOYEE

Well . . . every so often there'd be one a little off the path, right? They'd be right off the fucking *beaten track* in a few of 'em.

DARRELL

Such as?

EMPLOYEE

—ever had someone tongue your ass for ya? I mean, like, *maple syrup* outta there? Don't mean to be rude, but . . . (BEAT) Anyway. Shit 'a that nature.

DARRELL

I see.

EMPLOYEE

Dude can get chicks to do some pretty *off-the-wall* shit, seriously.

DARRELL

I bet—

EMPLOYEE

Yep. And this one time, time I saw your girlfriend . . . well, just pretty fucking startling. Quite.

DARRELL

Uh-huh. What? Go ahead—

EMPLOYEE

'S only about ten minutes long or so, but . . . (BEAT) You sure you . . .?
    (DARRELL *slowly nods yes. The* EMPLOYEE *puts down his broom.*)
Well, had no sex or whatever. No, yes, she does give him a little head, but . . . after that, *right* after, she sits up on the bed and kinda tilts back, like she's, I dunno, almost <u>waiting</u>. And he's pacing back and forth, kinda, you know, talking to himself. Then, outta nowhere, he justs turns on her and starts knocking the shit outta her. This guy does. In the stomach, punching her, maybe, twenty or thirty times. And hard! 'S a big dude

and she's gotta be, well, she's bawling and everything, so no doubt it fucking hurt. But she takes it. Gets back up each time and let's 'em do it again . . . well, then the tape ran out. Anyway, 's pretty out-there—

DARRELL

He hit her? That's all he did. *Hit* her.

EMPLOYEE

Yeah. That and the blow job, yeah. (BEAT) You okay?

DARRELL

—huh. (BEAT) Can you get me one?

EMPLOYEE

What? The tape . . . ?

DARRELL

Yeah.

EMPLOYEE

You smoking or what?! Fuck no, I told you, it's the dude's private *stock*. 'S a fucking serious customer, this guy—

DARRELL

Whatever.

EMPLOYEE

'S not, like, bootleg Pearl Jam footage, you know. Him fucking girls, and some underage shit at that. You're outta luck on that one—

DARRELL

Just asking.

EMPLOYEE

Right, but, you do not wanna mess with him. Promise.

DARRELL

Not a big issue. Anyway, thanks . . . I'll, uhhh, yeah.

EMPLOYEE

She said you'd wanna know, my cousin did, so I—

DARRELL

No problems. We're cool—

EMPLOYEE

—hey, you gonna get a dog or what?

DARRELL

Ahhh . . . I'll keep ya posted. Dunno.

EMPLOYEE

Whatever. We open at ten.

DARRELL *wanders off. The* EMPLOYEE *turns back to his cleaning, running the broom across the floor where* DARRELL *once was.*

THE LIVING ROOM

Same as before, maybe a bit messier. TV still on and loud. Today's newspaper on the sofa.

DARRELL *sits in a chair, looking straight ahead.* CAMMIE *is standing near* SHARI, *helping her into a coat. Baby cries in the other room.*

CAMMIE

—fucking fits, huh?

SHARI

Yeah.

CAMMIE

Good. Used to wear this all the time. 'S cute.

SHARI

It is, you're right.

CAMMIE

'Round the time I married your dad, I got this—

SHARI

Yeah? Well, I like the sleeves.

CAMMIE

Uh-huh.

SHARI (*to* DARRELL)

How do I look?

DARRELL

Nice.

SHARI

Thanks.

CAMMIE

Shit, he don't know! <u>Halston</u> came up and bit 'em on the ass, he wouldn't know.

SHARI

He likes it, though.

CAMMIE

Wears fucking *album* covers on his clothes, so I wouldn't put a bunch 'a stock in what Darrell thinks—

SHARI

Oh.

CAMMIE

Anyway, it's okay. Looks good on you. Way it's cut, shows off your butt—

SHARI

Not much 'a one.

CAMMIE

'S not bad. Filled out a little since the kid.

SHARI

Barely.

CAMMIE

Yeah, but a bit. Bit 'a something back there now—

SHARI

Thanks. You think?

CAMMIE

Shit yeah. Cute little ass! (*slaps it*) Even Darrell can see that much. Right? Darrell!

DARRELL

What?

CAMMIE

I said, "right"? Shari's ass looks okay, don't it?

DARRELL

Whatever.

CAMMIE

Shit. Moody little fucker . . . (*to* SHARI) Anyway, it does.
(*Baby cries out loudly.* SHARI *looks toward the hall
but* CAMMIE *waves her off as she yawns.*)
Worry 'bout it. I'll get 'em in a minute.

SHARI

Sure? I can—

CAMMIE

No, you two need to get going. Rich's gonna be in here in a
second, yelling and his usual show, so just go—

SHARI

'Kay. Thanks again.

CAMMIE

You bet.

SHARI

Won't stay late.

CAMMIE

No, no . . . long as you want.

SHARI

I don't like cars that much—

CAMMIE

Be nice, though. To get out. We saw 'em yesterday. Pretty
spectacular.

A car horn blasts. SHARI *turns and yells out the door.*

SHARI

Comin'!

CAMMIE *pushes a small wad of bills into* SHARI's *hand.* DARRELL *notices
this but says nothing, just laughs to himself.*

CAMMIE

Tell Rich to stop and get you some burgers. You didn't eat yet,
did ya?

SHARI

No.

CAMMIE

All right, then.

SHARI

You got milk, right? I forgot formula—

CAMMIE

'S about a half gallon. I'm gonna run out later.

SHARI

And he's got a little rash. I put some extra diapers in there . . . should be enough.

CAMMIE

Fine, no worries. Have some fun!

They hug briefly and then CAMMIE *crosses out to the hall and exits.* SHARI *grabs her purse and heads for the door.*

SHARI

—see ya, Darrell.

DARRELL

Yep.

SHARI

Have a good time tonight.

DARRELL

Thanks. You too.

SHARI

Yeah. (BEAT) You really think I look okay in this?

DARRELL (*turning finally*)

—uh-huh. Nice.

SHARI

And my ass? (*laughs*) 'S all right?

DARRELL

You look good.

SHARI

Then okay. So, better get out to the—

RICH *enters through the kitchen, looking a bit flustered.*

RICH

—fucking parking, huh?

SHARI

Yeah.

RICH

Need to get on the road, Shari, we want a shot at not walking for, like, *six* miles.

SHARI

I'm ready—

RICH

Good. Let's roll—

SHARI

'Kay.

RICH

Darrell. (BEAT) Darrell!

DARRELL

Yeah.

RICH

Answer a person, they fucking try to *communicate* with ya.

DARRELL

Sorry.

RICH

Tell your mother I can't back the Impala out for her. Don't know where the keys are—

DARRELL

Okay.

RICH

Maybe you can run down, pick up some milk for her. Don't really want her driving it, anyway, 'til I get it looked at.

DARRELL

Fine. Gotta get some smokes, anyhow—

RICH

Great. See ya. (*to* SHARI) Let's do it.

SHARI

Alright. Bye, Darrell.

DARRELL

So long.

SHARI *waves at* DARRELL *and* RICH *closes the door behind them.* DARRELL *sits by himself, staring at the TV. After a moment,* CAMMIE *returns. Baby is still crying*

CAMMIE

—fucking brat, huh?

DARRELL

Yeah.

CAMMIE

Cannot get 'em to calm down right now. Fuck it, cry m'self out. Whatever.

DARRELL

Right.

She yawns loudly.

CAMMIE

Ooommmmm! 'Nother hour, I'm not gonna hear shit, anyway, blubber away all he wants to . . . (BEAT) Time you taking off for your "big" thing?

DARRELL

Half hour or so—

CAMMIE

Alright. Where you guys going?

DARRELL

Just around.

CAMMIE

Sounds fun—

DARRELL

Yep.

They sit silently for a moment, watching the TV.

CAMMIE

Hate this fucking show—

DARRELL

Change it.

CAMMIE

Cable's out.

DARRELL

Oh.

CAMMIE

Yeah.

DARRELL

Fuck.

CAMMIE

Exactly. Don't matter, couldn't *hear* it over that little shit, anyway . . . (*yawns again*) Gonna lay down a minute.

DARRELL

'Kay.

CAMMIE

Wake me 'fore you go, alright? 'Least tell me you're off—

DARRELL

I will.

CAMMIE *stands and heads toward the hall.*
Hey, Mom?

CAMMIE

Yeah?

DARRELL

You really don't remember those forts we used to make on the
porch? I mean, with that blanket 'a yours—

CAMMIE

Nah, I really don't.

DARRELL

Huh.

CAMMIE

I can see that house in my head and all, but not so much specif-
ically about it. 'S a bad time for me, you know, just married and
I was pregnant, too, 'member? Yeah. Lost the kid, though, that
summer I lost it and Shari's dad and me at each other a lot.
Fighting. (BEAT) Not, like, the <u>best</u> chapter for me, so, you're
on your own with the *Kodak memories* and shit—

DARRELL

No big deal. Just asking—

CAMMIE

Truthfully, I don't recall that much about you. Really. Growing up, I mean.

DARRELL

No?

CAMMIE

Nah. Just fucking happened and then, one day, well, there you were. Darrell. (BEAT) Course I can remember taking you around places when you were little, the store and stuff, and losing you at the mall one time—Shopping Center, they used to call it, "Shopping Center"—you crawled under a god-damn bench outside Sears and I couldn't find you for, maybe, twenty minutes . . . Shit like that I recall, but you, I mean, just you as an individual—you never really made that big an impression—

CAMMIE *yawns and exits the room.* DARRELL *looks back to the TV. Tries the remote. Nothing. He stands now, going to the console and wiggling a wire in the back. Still nothing. Suddenly, he smacks the side of the set savagely several times. Like magic, a sharp picture appears.*

Satisfied, DARRELL *checks his watch and returns to his chair. He begins clicking through the channels, one after the next, faster and faster.*

THE PENGUIN POOL

Plexiglass wall set on a concrete barrier which separates the animals from visitors to the zoo. A pond, thin layer of ice on it, surrounds a replica of an iceberg. An EXHIBIT CLOSED FOR REPAIRS *sign taped to the glass.*

TIM *and* JENN *stand shivering in the dark, smoking. After a moment,* DARRELL *appears with a large canvas bag in his arms.*

DARRELL

—fucking fence, huh?

TIM

Yeah.

DARRELL

Tore the sleeve 'a my jacket all to shit! 'S fucking great—

JENN

It's cold.

TIM

The hell we doing <u>here</u>, anyway?

DARRELL

Just thoughta this, wanna show you something. (*looking around*) 'S fun here, ain't it? I get off on this place!

JENN

Darrell, I'm froze. What do you gotta show us so bad, couldn't do it *indoors*?

DARRELL

Take a minute, that's all—

TIM

Let's do it, then. (BEAT) They got guards come by every so often, you know.

TIM *looks around, worried.* DARRELL *smiles, kneeling to put the bag on the ground. He motions for* TIM *and* JENN *to have a look. Long silence as they stare into the bag, dumbfounded.*

JENN

—Darrell.

TIM

What is this?

DARRELL

Like you guys to meet someone.

TIM

Fucking *nephew.* Oh, man—

DARRELL

<u>Step</u>. 'S my step-nephew, and I thought we'd show 'em the sights.

JENN

Darrell, this is not funny.

DARRELL

Not being all jokey about this . . . took 'em for a ride, get 'em the hell outta the house! 'S mom drops him off our place, don't give a shit, so, here he is—

TIM *pokes gently at the bag.*

TIM

Sleeping.

DARRELL

Believe that? All the way from my house. *Resilient* little fuck, gotta give 'em that.

JENN

Too cold, this kinda shit, Darrell—

TIM

Seriously. Freezing my ass off in this *uniform*—

DARRELL

Rich said you could go a long way, trunk of a car, you warm enough. Thought maybe he was shitting me—

TIM *and* JENN *look at one another, trying to decide the best way to approach this.*

TIM

—yeah. (BEAT) 'S funny, you're right, going to the zoo with 'em, but it's just <u>way</u> too cold. Plus, his mom, huh?

DARRELL

Fuck his mom. What's she know, taking off the car show she's so goddamn worried?

JENN

Hey, Darrell, I'm tired, okay? You guys picked me up late, I'm cold and I wanna party and you're doing, just, like, *weird* shit now . . . so, thanks for the terrific birthday, let's drive back to your place or <u>something</u>. But not out *here*. All right?

JENN *picks up her purse and walks off.* TIM *starts to follow.*

TIM

Come on, dude, let's pack it up. Kid's gonna catch cold, be paying doctor's bills we're not careful.

DARRELL

—I wanna ransom him. Serious.

TIM *and* JENN *stop short.*

TIM

Huh? I don't get what you're—

JENN

This is what you wanna <u>show</u> me, Darrell? Is it?! 'Cause I ain't fucking *amused*.

DARRELL

What, you think I can't get anything in trade for this kid, 's that the matter?

TIM

No . . . dude—

JENN

'S a fucking <u>crime</u>, Darrell! That's the fucking *matter*!!

DARRELL

So?

JENN

What're you gonna do, call his mom, ask for a *million* bucks? F.B.I. on your ass in about twenty minutes—

TIM

—tops.

JENN

Be serious.

DARRELL

Think I'm playing fucking *Scrabble*?! I <u>am</u> serious—

TIM

You really ain't kidding, I mean, you're not, are you, Darrell?

JENN

I can't even . . . (*kneels down to the bag*) 'S cheeks are flushed.

TIM *comes over and takes a look as well. The baby begins to whimper.*

TIM

Too fucking brisk, this sorta shit. (BEAT) Damnit! Hell you gotta do it for, Darrell?!

DARRELL

Just <u>because</u> . . .
       (DARRELL *reaches down and scoops up the bag.*)
. . . now let's do it. Come on.

JENN

Darrell . . . fuck. She is not gonna give you nothing for that kid! Think about it.

DARRELL

Who?

JENN

The mother!!

DARRELL

I said "fuck her." 'S not <u>about</u> her. (BEAT) I wanna ransom 'em to you. You and Tim.

Silence as TIM *and* JENN *let this one sink in.* DARRELL *slowly zips the bag shut.*

TIM

—huh?

JENN

'S that supposed to mean?

DARRELL

Gonna play a game here, 'kay? (BEAT) Now, Jenn answers my questions, 's all cool. Tim can have the baby. You don't, and . . . well, I dunno what.
> (TIM *makes a move toward* DARRELL *and* DARRELL *fakes a toss to him. The whimper becomes a thin cry that floats off into the night.* TIM *stops dead.*)

. . . prefer a game of *catch*, instead?!

TIM

Darrell—

DARRELL

Huh?! Bet you get a hell of a *spiral* off this little bastard—

DARRELL *shakes the bag.* JENN *puts a hand to her mouth as* TIM *steps slowly back.*

JENN

Darrell . . . come on, please. Stop it, just fucking <u>stop</u>—

DARRELL (*stopping*)

—'kay. You guys ready now? Huh?

TIM

Yeah.

JENN

—yes.

DARRELL

Good. (BEAT) So . . . the fuck is going on?

TIM *and* JENN *try to remain calm, thinking quickly as to what* DARRELL *is after.*

> JENN

I dunno what you're trying to—

> DARRELL

Bullshit. <u>Bull</u>shit! Now don't . . . just *tell* me.

> TIM

Darrell—

> DARRELL

Yeah, what?

> JENN

I don't under<u>stand</u>, 'kay? The fuck do you want me to say?! Just gimme a—

> DARRELL

The truth! Fucking <u>truth</u>, some antique word I know, but I'm listening . . . (BEAT) Who the fuck was the *nigger*, two summers ago? Tell me now.

> TIM

This is—

> JENN

Oh fuck.

> DARRELL

Yeah, no kiddin', "oh fuck." You think all the shit you do just disappears into the *ether* somewheres, you keep it hidden long enough?

> JENN

—no, I just—

> DARRELL

What? <u>What?!</u>

> TIM

Darrell . . . listen to me, I was—

> JENN

He was this . . . shit, I don't know how to—

> TIM

—Jenn, lemme try to—

DARRELL

The black guy whose dick you sucked. His <u>basement</u>. 'S that help?! (BEAT) He made a video 'a the two of you—

JENN

—huh?

DARRELL

Yeah, "huh?" Same exact fucking thing I said . . . huh? Not Jenn, not my goddamn <u>girl</u>friend I left for three months 'cause my fucking mother sent me away, that can't be *her* giving this guy head!

JENN

You saw it?

TIM

Darrell—

DARRELL

Tim, shut the fuck up a second, <u>we're</u> talking now . . . (*to* JENN) No, I did not see it, but seems like I got a pretty good handle on the thing, don't it?

JENN

Yeah.

DARRELL

So, what, I just wasn't enough for ya, or, like, come on, go ahead, tell me—

JENN

'S not that.

DARRELL

—what is it about your *particular* legs, I wonder, makes 'em spread so fucking easy?
(TIM *takes another step toward* DARRELL, *who moves back and swings the bag wildly.*)
Fuck you doing, man, making your move?! You don't got the <u>balls</u>, Timmy! Not nearly enough!!

TIM *holds up his hands, backing off again.*

TIM

Be cool . . . cool it—

JENN

Darrell!

DARRELL

You're like, getting outta hand, you know that, Tim? 'Coming a <u>force</u> to be reckoned with, some shit like that!

TIM

Just don't, dude, 'cause I'm trying to talk this through and you're fucking with me! <u>Don't!!</u>

DARRELL *pretends to drop the bag. Does it again.*

DARRELL

What're you gonna do?! Huh?! Come on!!

JENN

Stop it! Stop!! (BEAT) I'll tell you, I will, just <u>STOP!!!</u>
    (TIM *backs down first, then* DARRELL. DARRELL
    turns and stares straight at JENN, *who is tearing
    up now.*)
'S that what this is about? Huh? All this . . . <u>shit</u> . . . 's about that?!

DARRELL

No. Never really liked the kid . . . glad I did this. (BEAT) Now, hurry up.

JENN

—I don't know about any tapes, nothing like that. I don't.

DARRELL

Uh-huh—

JENN

He was just this guy I . . . met. This one guy. That summer you took off and we broke up, all your stuff about "no strings" and, you know, whatever. That's when.

DARRELL

You . . . you know I never mean that shit—

JENN

Yeah, well, you said <u>it!</u> Said it to me and there I am, June or whatever, and I come to find out ya left me a little *present*. Yeah. Carrying it around, which, at fifteen, is just <u>not</u> gonna happen. So I found a way to get rid of the thing—

DARRELL

I don't get it. What're you saying?

JENN

Fuck, Darrell—

DARRELL

<u>What?</u>

JENN

You got me *pregnant*. Had to do something!
          (DARRELL, *still clutching the bag, stands there*
          blinking and trying to process.)
. . . <u>had</u> to, and you nowhere in sight.

DARRELL

Oh.

TIM

'S my fault.

DARRELL

Tim, I told you to stay the fuck—

TIM

No, man, you're gonna listen to me! I been taking your shit,
playground 'a elementary school since, and you're gonna fucking hear me out!! Just *listen* to me, Darrell . . . I said, 's <u>my</u>
fault. (BEAT) I'm the one who gave Jenn his name—

DARRELL

You did? <u>You?</u>

TIM

Yes.

DARRELL

And why's that? Tim, huh? (BEAT) Why would you do some
shit like that to me?—

TIM

'Cause. Look, the guy . . . he helped my sister out. Used to go
with her, they were both seniors at Washington. Got her
knocked up once and she told me, a while after that, he beat
her in the stomach when they knew. He did it with another
girl, too, or something. Anyway, he <u>knew</u> how it's done, and so
she told me about it . . . 's all I could come up with!

JENN

'S true. You weren't around so I asked Tim for help—

DARRELL

—I see—

JENN

—he gave me the name and whatever happened happened. It got done.

TIM

Right.

JENN

Don't know about this tape . . . honest. I did it because I was three months in and I was scared. That's the whole fuckin' tale—

DARRELL *is silent.* TIM *takes a step forward.*

DARRELL

—and you couldn't say a word to me, huh? I mean, fuck . . . (*to* TIM) *Neither* one 'a you?

JENN

Darrell—

DARRELL

Two fucking years since and you couldn't maybe just drop a little *hint*?!

JENN

Yeah, you're right, that woulda been great . . . fuck, Darrell, you start *yelling* I glance at some guy too long, cover 'a People magazine!!

DARRELL

Whatever. (BEAT) And I suppose . . . you gave him head because . . .?

JENN

Jesus, Darrell, because I didn't-have-any-money! What do you think?!! 'S what he *charged* me so I did it!!!

DARRELL

—oh. Oh.

They all stand for a moment in a bit of a standoff. JENN *finally puts her hands out.*

JENN

—there. Now gimme the kid.

TIM

I'm asking nice, now, Darrell . . . I had it with this kinda shit!
Put 'em <u>down</u>. Just do it, man . . . said you would.

DARRELL *stops and smiles. He lets out a deep breath and motions with one hand, holding the bag out.*

DARRELL

Yeah, the fuck was I thinking? Here—

TIM *slowly reaches for the bag. At the last moment,* DARRELL *pulls it back and lets it fly with a full revolution over the top of the penguin fence. A soft plop! and it is gone.*

For a second, TIM *and* JENN *stand frozen where they are, unable to move, then* TIM *suddenly makes a run at the fence.*

TIM

NO!

JENN

Oh my God!!

TIM *tries to climb the wall but* DARRELL *pulls him back down.*

TIM

—the fuck off me!!

DARRELL

Whooaah, Timmy!! Getting a little big, your fucking britches—

TIM

Fuck! Fucker!! Fuck <u>you</u>, Darrell!!!

DARRELL

Come on! Do it, ya stupid motherfucker!! <u>Stupid!!!</u>

At this, TIM *lunges at* DARRELL *and pins him to the ground, pounding away at him.* DARRELL *throws the bigger boy off him and starts to tear at* TIM's *face.* JENN *jumps in at this, trying to protect* TIM. DARRELL *throws her off and goes back to scratching* TIM.

TIM *crawls out from under* DARRELL *and kicks his friend savagely in the gut.* DARRELL *doubles over and* TIM *pounds away.* DARRELL *drops to one knee, knocking over a garbage can.* TIM *follows after* DARRELL, *who comes up with the can lid and smashes it across* TIM's *face.* TIM *goes down hard.*

TIM

Aaaaaahhh!

DARRELL *beats him a few more times with it until he is silent.* JENN *tries to intervene again and is hit hard on the arm and shoulder for her troubles.*

DARRELL *finally falls back, bloody and breathing hard. He throws the lid loudly onto the sidewalk.* JENN *huddles near the crumpled, silent body of* TIM.

DARRELL

—fucking done, huh?

JENN

Yeah.

DARRELL

Not gonna bring the loveable little *tyke* back, none 'a this shit—

JENN

That baby . . . oh my god—

DARRELL *slowly gets to his feet, staggering a bit.* JENN *stays where she is, even when* DARRELL *offers a hand.*

DARRELL

Know what? Jenn? Know what we gotta do? Get the fuck out, outta this place. Got a car, take us anywhere we want. (*reaches in his pocket*) Look, even got my mom's Visa, so . . . you choose. Choose a place and I'm there. Seriously, just pick and . . . I don't care the distance from here. We'll go, 'kay? Just . . . Jenn. Tell me a place. Fuck. Jenn? Jenn! You pick . . . you—

JENN

No, Darrell . . . I don't think I can.

DARRELL

Come on!

JENN

—so fucking scared—

DARRELL

Jenn, I said "now!"

JENN

No, Darrell.

DARRELL

Oh. Oh, I see, I'm with ya—

JENN

Not gonna leave Tim—

DARRELL

I got it, you don't accept, huh? Don't wanna be part 'a the mess. That it?

JENN

No. Just ain't leaving.

DARRELL

Staying with ol' Timmy . . . 's fine. <u>Fine</u>. (BEAT) Guess he didn't turn out to be so fucking *stupid* after all, did he? No, not at all . . . well, well.
> (DARRELL *suddenly picks up the entire trashcan and holds it high over his head. He moves toward* TIM *but* JENN *throws her body across him, hands up trying to protect his face.*)

So, that's the end of our fucking story, huh? Yeah? (BEAT) Slit your belly open, all the guy's dicks been in there, never be able to see I even left a *mark*—

DARRELL *finally drops the can and moves off. Wanders.*

JENN

Darrell . . . wait—

DARRELL

Guess I'll just keep driving, you know? Go upstate, maybe, fuck if I know. Just run like rabbits. Headlights blasting, signposts whipping by, fucking squirrels and shit diving to get outta my way! Yeah, I like that. Got some plastic, might take me <u>anywhere</u>. And I don't give a fuck it's any place I ever even heard of—

With that he is gone. JENN *is left alone now with* TIM *in the quiet of the zoo. She slowly sits up, cradling* TIM's *head in her lap.*

THE LIVING ROOM

Same as earlier, with a few lamps turned on. The TV still noisy, this time with a World War II picture.

RICH *and* SHARI *together on the couch. He is pulling her close, kissing her, but* SHARI *keeps moving away slightly.*

RICH

—fucking tense, huh?

SHARI

Yeah. Can't help it.

RICH

I know.

SHARI

Fuck, this is . . . I dunno. I just—

RICH

What?

SHARI

Kinda see myself as shit, you know?

RICH

Right.

SHARI

I mean, lying to her, 'bout us, all this time.

RICH

Hey, you don't like it, then stop.

SHARI

No, I just—

RICH

'S pretty fucking simple. Not, like, no great *moral dilemma.*

SHARI

No—

RICH

Don't care for it . . . don't fucking do it.

He is close to her now, breathing on her cheek. She turns slowly and kisses him again.

SHARI

It's my *mom*, that's all.

RICH

<u>Step</u>. Step-mother—

SHARI

Still. Like some lump 'a shit, doing this to her.

RICH

Sure. (*kissing her*) Don't feel *that* bad, though. Does it?

SHARI

—no. Not <u>so</u> bad, I guess—

She continue to kiss, sliding her hand down into his pants.

RICH

—fucking nice, huh?

SHARI

Yeah.

RICH

Whatever you wanna call it—"wrong," some kind 'a *betrayal*, fine—it's still nice, ain't it?

SHARI

It's very nice.

A car goes past and SHARI *looks up, nervous. She pulls her hand back out of* RICH'*s jeans.*

RICH

Easy, 's alright. Said she was gonna run down the 7-11, see if she can spot Darrell. That's, like, *miles* away—

SHARI

Sure?

RICH

Uh-huh.

SHARI

'Kay. (BEAT) And you think, I mean, he's got the baby, right? I'm sure he does, but—

RICH

Absolutely. No question . . . it's fine. (BEAT) Don't even know who the dad is, right, so don't worry so much—

For emphasis, RICH *shoots a hand up under her blouse. She doesn't fight it.*

SHARI

Yeah. You wanna take a blood test?

RICH

That's not so funny—

SHARI

—kinda.

RICH

Uh-huh. (*kisses her*) Know what I'd like? Tell you the truth, like more than any one thing? Say to your step-mom, "Go to Hell!" and move my shit outta here, take up with you . . . Huh? Be great! Two incomes, I mean, your welfare and my job, got a kid already—

SHARI

Could have more—

RICH

We could. We could do that. Do whatever the fuck it is we felt. Build a deck, the back 'a your duplex if we wanted, pack up and take the baby to *Oregon*, a fucking vacation, we had the mind to do it. (BEAT) That's what I'd like to do . . . just be with you.

Long silence as they kiss again, RICH *pawing at her as they go.*

SHARI

Be so great . . . to be together. You know, like you said, but to do something really different, too. I mean, some kinda thing that nobody'd expect outta us. You and me. (BEAT) Maybe add a deck, or a patio, a kinda addition you was taking about, only paint the house at the same time. <u>But</u> . . . right down the middle, where the two front doors are. And use some color that'd drive the whole neighborhood crazy! Maroon, maybe, or a real splashy kind, like a *magenta*. Sorta shade you'd never use on a house . . . but we would.

She continues to kiss him as she speaks.

Landlord'd get a bunch 'a complaints, just people driving by, screaming their heads off. City council in an uproar, all kinds 'a *court actions* against us . . . and we'd stay holed up inside, drapes all pulled shut, baby can't even go to school when he grows up 'cause kids'd attack 'em on the playground! And you and me can't get to the car to go to work, or the store, nothing. We all gotta just stay inside. Food running out. Utilities all been shut off. And so . . . we just make love all the time. Day and night. 'Cause that's all we got left. (BEAT) That's what I want, Rich—

She finishes speaking and they kiss again fully. After a moment they break and RICH *sits up, lighting a cigarette.*

RICH

Me too, honey . . . I could handle that.

SHARI

Yeah?

RICH

You bet. (BEAT) But hey, who gives two shits what we want, right?

A car door slams. RICH *gets up and crosses to a counter, finding an ashtray.* SHARI *runs a hand through her hair.*

CAMMIE *enters, a bag of groceries in her arm. She comes in and moves to the kitchen to unload.*

SHARI

—fucking late, huh?

RICH

Yeah.

CAMMIE

Just wish it wasn't so late. Wouldn't worry so much.

RICH

'S okay. (BEAT) So, nothing?

SHARI

Nope.

SHARI

You didn't see 'em anywhere, Cammie? Darrell, I mean?

CAMMIE

Uh-uh. Drove past most the places I know he and Tim hang out, but—

RICH

Huh. 'S got a job, that Tim does—

CAMMIE

I checked. They ain't seen 'em.

SHARI

Oh—

RICH

Come on, there's an explanation for all this! I know there is—

CAMMIE

I did not lose no newborn—

SHARI

'Course not.

RICH

No way.

CAMMIE

Don't need to worry until you got a reason. Let's just wait'll Darrell gets home, 'kay?

SHARI

—sure.

CAMMIE

He comes in and there's nothing, then maybe we gotta call the cops. Or I dunno.

SHARI

Yeah, he probably knows what's going on. I'm sure—

RICH

Kid's gonna show up. No problem. (BEAT) I bet Darrell took 'em out in the Impala, get some smokes or that kinda setup. A fucking *Slurpee*—

SHARI *nods her head in silence.*

CAMMIE

'S it, I promise you anything—

SHARI

I'm sure that's right. Yeah. <u>Something</u> just like that.

CAMMIE *is standing in the kitchen archway and* RICH *gives her a little peck on the cheek. She smiles and moves off.*

CAMMIE

Good. Gonna make some coffee, then—

RICH *moves back to the couch, ashtray in hand.* SHARI *leans over and steals a puff,* RICH *keeping a lookout. She tries to go for more now, a kiss, but* RICH *stops her cold.*

RICH

Maybe you should give your *mom* a little help . . . she's pretty
tired.

SHARI *stares at* RICH, *then stands and starts off. He smacks! her hard across the backside as she passes.* RICH *just smiles at her, then turns away to finish his smoke.*

THE WALL OF THE ZOO

High cement barricade that stretches off into the distance. Withered foliage can be seen behind. A covered bench in front. Weather-beaten CITY BUS SCHEDULE *sign nearby.*

Time has passed. Snow is falling, a dusting on everything in sight. Not a soul around.

JENN *and* TIM *stand near the wall.* JENN *holds a towel.* TIM *sits pulling down his socks. His shoes are already off.*

TIM

—not so bad, huh?

JENN

Yeah.

TIM

I felt a lot worse'n this. Used to go running, I was a kid, you
know, what'd they call it, *streaking*. Me and some other guys—
Darrell'd do it—nothing on. So, this ain't so bad.

JENN

But, Tim . . . why don't you just keep your clothes on 'til you're in there, take 'em off over by the thing? The penguin pool.

TIM

'Cause. 'S Sunday, <u>supposed</u> to be closed, but who knows? Some dude in there, gives chase or whatever . . . I'm not leaving shit behind. You got my stuff out *here*. See?

JENN

Oh, okay. Got it.

TIM

'S just my <u>plan</u> . . . I'm only going in, a few minutes, anyway.

JENN

Fine.

They look at each other for a moment, then TIM *strips off his pants. He stands now in his T-shirt and briefs.*

TIM

You hear from Darrell yet?

JENN

No.

TIM

Huh, me either.

JENN

I don't care. It's better—

TIM

—I been coming here a lot lately, all the time. Not really checking or nothing, but, you know.

JENN

I do, too. Sometimes.

TIM

I mean, once the cops talked to us and all, figured it was safe . . . (BEAT) They all think that Darrell's got the—

JENN

—I know. Yeah.

TIM

Anyway, I come here, walk around and . . . whatever. You can still see the mark.

JENN

Barely.

TIM

Yeah, but you can still see it. Never actually freezes completely over again, something breaks through a sheet 'a ice.

JENN

Really?

TIM

Yep. Learned that in science.

JENN

Huh. Looked like it mighta got more round, you know? The hole. Like it's more rounded—

TIM

Yeah. It is, from the water lapping at it. It's rounder. Almost, like a perfect circle.

JENN

Right.

TIM *studies* JENN *for a moment, then moves to her.*

TIM

—I was . . . after, at home, woke up with a fucking ache, you know, <u>head</u>ache, like nothing else. But I was okay. 'Cept, every so often, I'm walking down the street, could be anywhere, and I'm suddenly taken over, right? Like, just where I'm standing . . . middle of a school crosswalk, doesn't matter. I get taken up by these *visions*. 'S like, I dunno, I can see all this shit. I'm sorta standing knee-deep in water, with forests just sprouting up all around, and kinda palaces in the distance. And I'm there with all this other stuff, too, top 'a the water but I can see underwater, the same time! Spot all manner 'a ocean creatures. Like them 3-D books they had, you're in grade school, dinosaurs and whatever, you can see the air and the land <u>and</u> under the sea. That's what it's like. And I'm just, you know, knocked out by it! I don't know what's happening, so I reach out, stop one 'a these water people, a beautiful young girl and I casually say, "the fuck's go ing on?" And she doesn't know. She doesn't, just this big smile at me and then swims off. You believe that? It's like a fantasy, but it really exists, too, the same time. Kind 'a *comforting*. And so, in this dream, I just start swimming, right, out with all these trees around and kingdoms and big mother hammerheads coming up and *nuzzling* me. And after a while, I forget that I don't swim so good. I just keep paddling. All the time going farther and farther out in the water, but going under, too . . . deeper and deeper. And you know what? I have, like, absolutely <u>no</u> idea the fuck's going on . . . but I'm having the *time* of my life.

Suddenly TIM *feels as if he's said too much; he grows quiet.* JENN *puts a hand on his shoulder.*

JENN

—I've had the same kinda dream.

TIM

You're shitting me.

JENN

No. It's like that . . . not all that stuff, but a lot 'a things are very similar.

TIM

Huh. What do you think 'a that?

JENN

I dunno.

TIM *quickly pulls his T-shirt over his head.*

TIM

Well, I'm gonna go now. Stand here all fucking day, right?

JENN

Right.

TIM

—'s a good thing to do, ain't it, Jenn? I mean, going in there?

JENN

I think so—

TIM

I know we swore not to tell nobody and shit, get us into trouble, but I don't like it much . . . that kid just down under water there. All this time. I don't—

JENN

Me neither.

TIM

Okay, then. (BEAT) You be here with the towel?

JENN

I'm right here—

TIM

All right.
>   (TIM *crosses to the wall, but stops and looks back*
>   *at* JENN.)
Hey, Jenn?

JENN

Yeah?

TIM

Tell me honest . . . you don't think this is, like, <u>stupid</u>, do ya?

JENN

No, I don't, Tim. (BEAT) I don't think it's stupid at all—

TIM

—that's good.

TIM *turns and quickly scrambles up the wall. He perches on top for a long moment, taking in a few sharp breaths.* TIM *smiles back at* JENN, *then jumps over the other side.*

JENN *stands alone now, looking up. She clutches the towel.*

SILENCE. DARKNESS.